AUTHOR

BAILEY, A

CLASS

F   H

M

TITLE

Major Andre

1928

D1321314

Major André

BOOKS BY ANTHONY BAILEY

FICTION
Making Progress (1959)
The Mother Tongue (1961)
Major André (1987)

NONFICTION
The Inside Passage (1965)
Through the Great City (1967)
The Thousand Dollar Yacht (1968)
The Light in Holland (1970)
In the Village (1971)
A Concise History of the Low Countries (1972)
Rembrandt's House (1978)
Acts of Union (1980)
Along the Edge of the Forest (1983)
Spring Jaunts (1986)

AUTOBIOGRAPHY
America, Lost & Found (1981)
England, First & Last (1985)

ANTHONY BAILEY

MAJOR ANDRE

CARCANET

First published in Great Britain in 1989 by
Carcanet Press Limited
208–212 Corn Exchange Buildings
Manchester M4 3BQ

British Library Cataloguing in Publication Data
Bailey, Anthony,   1933–
Major Andre.
I. Title
823'.914[F]

ISBN 0-85635-795-2

The Publisher acknowledges financial assistance from
the Arts Council of Great Britain

Printed in Great Britain by SRP Ltd., Exeter

Major André

PROLOGUE

Much later, when he had become a Member of Congress, Benjamin Tallmadge would look back on that particular time as that in which his country's fortunes were at their most precarious point of balance, ready to be pushed fatefully one way or the other. It was also the point at which his own military service came to signify more in his life than merely an accumulated number of years volunteered to the American cause—so that, a Connecticut schoolteacher before the Revolution, a civilian (you would have thought) to the core, he was ever afterwards honoured to be addressed by the title Colonel (the rank he held at the close of hostilities), and to recall from time to time for close acquaintances and family his small part in those momentous happenings. "Once a soldier, always a soldier," he would say, flicking dust from his boots, or, possibly set going on his recollections by an act of public scandal or deceit, "A proper soldier would not act that way." Certainly his service gave him the right (which he did not overindulge) to sound like a veteran.

It might also be the coming of autumn that set his memories in train. The leaves would begin to turn. A friend, or a child, would become the audience for whom he suddenly found a need—close enough to him that he did not have to remind them that, aged twenty-four, he had been called to the colours almost at the start in 1776 and had served with the First Connecticut Regiment from its formation. He might, however, broadly sketch the shifts that occurred in the following four years—here success, here failure; the Continental cause seeming to lose the battles but somehow not altogether lose the campaigns—before arriving at the time that most concerned him, September 1780.

"I was at North Castle, a forward post in Westchester, New York, serving as second-in-command to Lieutenant Colonel Jameson of Sheldon's Dragoons, with a number of Connecticut militia attached. Our main army, some ten thousand men, was encamped at Tappan, on the western side of Hudson's river. Our allies, the French, had not long before occupied Rhode Island and—following Lafayette's advice to accept General Washington's supreme command—stood ready to assist us. The French fleet had at last taken from the British their complete sway of the sea. In regard to lines of communication between us and the French, we held control of the important river crossing at West Point, where General Arnold commanded. Thus, in the North we felt that we were keeping pressure on the King's armies, while apparently losing ground in the Southern states. There the British had taken Charleston earlier in the year. Lord Cornwallis had recently beaten General Gates at Camden. Our hopes lay in the fact that the Carolina countryside was by no means sympathetic to the Royal forces, and it may have been as unclear to Earl Cornwallis as it was to us where he would march next.

"Matters were not much more certain in the

Prologue

Northern sphere. General Clinton—Sir Henry Clinton —was the British commander in chief, with his headquarters and most of his troops, twenty thousand strong, on New York island. His fleet lay in Gardiner's bay, at the eastern end of Long Island. We had been expecting Clinton to move against the French on Rhode Island, using his fleet for that purpose, but from reports I had been receiving from the city, from our informers there, it appeared that he was concerned that our forces were preparing to attack New York. General Washington was no doubt pleased to encourage this anxiety. Congress, as I recall, was then in its wisdom prompting our commander to attack Canada —which would of course have removed the pressure on Sir Henry! Other difficulties worth remembering are that we were in a bad way for provisions and clothing. In terms of food, too many American farmers had become soldiers. Our money was nearly valueless. I remember being asked to pay a hundred Continental dollars for a new handkerchief—a single handkerchief! Needless to say, I made do with what I had.

"In mid-September, at North Castle, I was told that General Washington was going to Hartford to confer with the French commander Rochambeau. I also had word from New York that Sir George Rodney had just sailed in from the West Indies with nearly a dozen ships of the line. This, I believed, suggested trouble. Clinton's naval colleague Admiral Arbuthnot had shown no signs of initiative or aggression, but of Rodney we understood otherwise: he was a fighter— something like Arnold on land was for us. Moreover, the additional ships Rodney brought gave Sir Henry naval control again. It gave him the wherewithal to strike. Little did we guess how and where he meant to do so! Little did I suppose that I would be intimately involved with his scheme, or should I say its aftermath? It all remains exceptionally vivid for me, from the night when I returned to North Castle from a patrol down to the White Plains and found Colonel Jameson in some confusion, to the days at Tappan, not long after, when I became acquainted more intimately with Major John André. I remember the short path that led through the front yard to the house in Tappan, and the shape of the latch that opened the door."

TAPPAN

Thursday, September 28

1780

Ah, Tallmadge—do come in. Don't smile. I still stand on ceremony. You mustn't think it foolish if a captive talks to his captors with a concern for etiquette. It may be the one thing that keeps him going. And I was brought up that way. You know, I have spent the last hour, since arriving here, in examining this room. It gives me an awful feeling of being my last room, I'm not quite sure why. Perhaps simply from being in so many different rooms in these past days—though I've lodged in worse than this. Four strides by three. The window has a view down the garden and beyond to that hill with the three trees. I cannot see your lines, but I heard some fifes and drums just now. Is the great man arrived? Will he take part in my proceedings? No, I know you aren't permitted to answer that. But I will need to rehearse my case, such as it is. And it would be pleasant to talk to you. I didn't feel that I could, while riding here from West Point, with that dreadful fellow Smith along—I hope you're keeping him in chains. Has he turned King's evidence, or whatever you call it? Congress's evidence doesn't have quite the same ring. That's if he really did understand what he had got himself into, and I'm not sure he did. Or if

I did! Part of my trouble has been lack of sleep. I find it hard to sort out in my head the various stages of my errand, to fix precisely where things went wrong. I thought that generally I was obeying my instructions —and yet. It feels curiously like a dream. I keep thinking that I am going to wake up from it, shivering and shaking, and find myself back in New York, or at least back on board the *Vulture*. Perhaps I'll find the affair hasn't even started yet! This is just a nightmare. In real life it will be different.

Do you remember as a boy falling into a sort of doze during afternoon lessons—summer afternoons especially? You said you were a schoolteacher before the Rebellion, or the hostilities, as you no doubt prefer to call it, so you'll have seen the phenomenon from both sides, pupil's desk and teacher's lectern. How hard it was sometimes not to drop off—and then the swish of a cane! Harsh punishment for so natural an offense. In the past week I have been prevented from sleeping, kept up at night, or else so full of apprehension that sleep has been impossible. It may be, in consequence, that I start to rattle on a little. I was quite naturally taciturn when we first met, and I was still in my role as Mr. John Anderson. I didn't want to overplay the indignation I ought to have felt at being stopped. And if I begin to make up for my previous speechlessness, it may perhaps be because of a feeling that I will need a spokesman, someone to deliver a report to my fellow men, a *rapporteur*. Of course I remember that it is young Hamilton who speaks French, and not you, Major. But nurture and blood will out. I spent a few years in Geneva as a boy, when my father's business took him back there. What age is Hamilton, anyway— twenty-five? Only a few years younger than you. I am a year senior to you, I recall. Thirty and four months. The thought intrudes that I will not be thirty and five months. I think it is best to let these thoughts rise to the surface if they must.

I must remind myself to speak with caution when it affects my fellow officers and the service. Since you have been doing a similar job to mine, in some ways, you'll understand this—you know how we try to weave a tapestry of fact from snippets of information. If I talk, it is partly in the hope of informing myself. Although you might suspect it, I have no desire to be instrumental in Arnold's return to you. I imagine your commander has speculated about this, and even perhaps opened a negotiation through which an exchange might be proffered—Arnold for me. I can tell him, it would be without point. Sir Henry Clinton, my chief, would not begin to consider it. Oh, Sir Henry will shed some tears for John André. But I fear there are limits placed by honour and military responsibility on what he will be able to do.

I had tried to set up a meeting with your dashing Major General several weeks before this present escapade, but he did not turn up. A correspondence to the same end had been conducted for some time. It seems to me that it is a proper object in war, to take advantage of a rebel officer's desire to return to his proper allegiance, don't you think? Part of the case for the defense! Our letter writing was made easier by the fact that we had friends in common in Philadelphia. Sometimes we used cipher, picking words out of an agreed volume and indicating what they were by giving numbers for page, line, and position of word in the line. Blackstone's *Commentaries on the Laws of England* was a favoured text. Nicely chosen—a legal instrument in the effort to put down a rebellion. I admit that I hoped this correspondence would bring about an event—a turning point. Don't laugh! I know that on both sides we hunger for turning points. In this case, it seemed to be no fanciful dream but a main chance. Your man, if I may call him that, was the most aggressive commander in the field—more forceful and daring than any of ours, when it comes to it. Well worth the having. And the thought that he might come over on an occasion when there could also be offered up a large body of troops and a strategic post, the key to the river, *that* seemed worth a deal of trouble and risk. I had dreams of glory, I suppose. If it had come off . . . There would have been no way in which Sir Henry could have refused me the command of the left wing during the assault on West Point. My chances of surviving would have been exceptionally high, as you realize. And the difficulties which Sir Henry has had with Whitehall in getting confirmation of my rank as major would have been shot clean away. Sir John André, at the least. My mother would have been proud.

It is Thursday today, isn't it? Then it is just a week since I was aboard the *Vulture*. There you are, Tallmadge—obviously in the wrong army, without an opportunity to appreciate the pleasures of life on shipboard. For myself, I prefer the river to the sea. Emphatically so. Going to Charleston last winter—going to Nantucket in the summer of '78—coming over in '74 —God, was I sick! How those vessels roll! It amazes me that we carry on a war three thousand miles from Britain with an ocean of headwinds and implacable seas to battle against with each cargo of orders, men, and equipment. Horses dying. Men dying. Pox and the plague below decks and the devil at the helm. You have it easier, Tallmadge, believe me. On the other hand, I acknowledge that I did not feel threatened by such hardships off Teller's Point last week. I came up in a smaller sloop from Dobb's Ferry with the tide on the Wednesday afternoon. Hudson's river eminently pleasant. I was in elated spirits. A sparkling September day. Hard to believe a war was being fought. The green wooded slopes of the river shore—a few boats fishing—perhaps they were your spy boats—and the *Vulture* in solitude at anchor on the eastern edge of the channel into Haverstraw bay. We reached her at sunset. I expected Arnold or an emissary from him to appear that night, but no one came. Colonel Robinson was already on board—Beverley Robinson, a Colonial officer loyal to the King, as you no doubt know. It seemed a good idea, with his great knowledge of the area and his own house, Robinson's House, across the river from West Point below Sugar Loaf Mountain, where General Arnold and his family were living. What more natural than communication between the owner of the house and its present resident about household problems. After supper Sutherland, the *Vulture*'s captain, passed the port around. His first lieutenant joined us for a game of whist. We talked about the occasion a month back when Sir Henry on board ship at Huntingdon thought he'd been poisoned. Arsenic in the mulligatawny! He firmly believed that your Jersey governor, Livingston, had instigated an attempt on his life. For myself, I suspected the clams, which he ate uncooked like oysters.

I couldn't sleep. That was the first night of insomnia in this little campaign of mine. I walked the quarter-deck under the mizzenmast. Stars above, to be seen through the rigging, but no reflection of them on the waters below because of the mist on the river. The master-at-arms also paced the deck. He told me that just before dusk one of the *Vulture*'s boats, patrolling between the ship and the shore, had seen a white flag being waved on the land. The boat went in to investigate, and was then fired on. Perhaps the noise of this incident frightened off Arnold's boat. The master-at-arms said that there were Yankee guard boats out as well. I could see little. The mist held like crystals whatever light there was in the darkness; there were no shapes, nothing of substance, only the shrouds shimmering in the moisture-filled air.

Yet that incident gave us an opening next morning. It helped our impatience, too. We sent a boat upriver under a flag of truce to complain to the American commander, General Arnold, about the false behaviour of the Rebels in decoying our boat ashore and then firing on it. This was not according to the rules of war. I remember thinking that at this point in the conflict even Colonial farmers should be aware of that. Sutherland put his signature to this letter, but I wrote it and countersigned it "John Anderson, Secretary." So Arnold should know that I was aboard. Then there was a long day of waiting. I assume your army is the same as ours in that respect, Tallmadge—a lot of charging back and forth and an even greater amount of dithering. I would like a guinea for every day I have spent inactive in this war, and not just while I was held prisoner in Pennsylvania. When our forces moved off in the campaign that led to the capture of Philadelphia we spent a week or so sitting aboard ships in New York harbour. When we went off to Charleston it was the same. On this occasion the circumstances

were quite comfortable. The vessel was not teeming
with soldiery. After breakfasting, I chatted with
Beverley Robinson. An interesting man, about twice
my age. He can go on a bit with his stories about
serving under Wolfe at Quebec, but on the subject of
the current—never-ending!—revolt, he is full of
matter. Beforehand he was very much against government policy, and yet he felt strongly against the
separation of the Colonies from Great Britain. I think
he and you, Tallmadge, would be well matched—he
knows as much about what is going on within your
lines as you, I believe, know about ours. He seemed to
enjoy being upriver, close to his house, which he
hadn't seen for several years.

And yet he was worried about our arrangements.
He thought we should have insisted that Arnold meet
us, on neutral ground, at Dobb's Ferry. He was perplexed when I told him that Arnold had wanted me to
come to his quarters at Robinson's House, though he
said with a laugh that I would then have been able to
find out whether the roof was still tight. Colonel
Robinson had heard most of the stories about Arnold,
and as a wealthy landowner clearly regarded your
General as an upstart, and untrustworthy. "You know
he held shares in privateers, or so I've been told," Robinson said. "And then there's this row he's been having
with Congress about his expenses. His fellow officers
don't seem altogether enchanted with the man, for
that matter." I acknowledged that if Arnold had not
managed to persuade General Washington to give him
the command of West Point, making much of his leg
injury received at Bemis Heights, Saratoga, then Sir
Henry would probably have decided against continuing our correspondence.

Major André

Captain Sutherland had been suffering from an attack of the ague during the morning, but he joined us for dinner in the afternoon. By the time the port and madeira made their evening rounds, he was generally more relaxed. Curt or cantankerous the rest of the time. We had one of those conversations I must have had with naval men a hundred times in the six years I've been on this continent. How at least forty thousand men were needed for a proper land war. And if they weren't provided, then it would be best to have a purely naval war. The main American ports strictly blockaded, the French fleet kept bottled up in the Mediterranean. Too many second-raters employed here now, since no one with ability cared to risk his reputation in this conflict. I reminded the good Captain (who by the way had led his ship in action most successfully against privateers) that Sir George Rodney had recently arrived from the Indies and was embarking troops in New York harbour at just that moment, while waiting for the word to come from the *Vulture* to proceed upriver. "Well, he'd better act promptly, before he goes ashore and is infected by fatal lassitude," said Sutherland. It is hard to find a naval officer who doesn't imagine that New York is a lotus land and that we army men are dilettantes and popinjays. Robinson didn't help at this point by suggesting that I could have put on for the Admiral a special performance at the John Street playhouse—Shakespeare's *Tempest*, perhaps. Sir Henry, he supposed, would by now have asked Sir George what instrument he played, with the hope of expanding the private Clinton trio into a quartet.

My own point of view had for a long time been that it made sense to concentrate on Hudson's river. Sir

Henry had had some of his successes here; here he had been bold and captured American forts. Of course Howe should never have shipped his army to Philadelphia in '77. If he had brought those men upriver to meet Burgoyne, there would never have been the disaster of Saratoga. Spilt milk, you'll say. Well, if we had held a firm line along the river, we could have kept the Colonies divided—Washington even now would have been unable to have made his way across country to confer with Rochambeau. As for West Point, it is the keystone of such a policy. I've heard it said that your Baron von Steuben appreciates this. Thus we had an opportunity to take it, to take the initiative, and end the war on fair terms.

I see you are nodding, Tallmadge. I presume you agree that it was an opportunity, even if you don't agree about the terms of our arrangement for acquiring it. What questions have you for me, then? My orders? That is a sensible query. Sir Henry left me some scope; you'll have seen what I did with it. But the first objective was to make contact with Major General Arnold, in order to ascertain that our understanding of his intentions was correct, and in order to assure him of our good faith. I had been given various other commands —or, one might say, restrictions and advice, for as you know, in the field orders have sometimes to be interpreted in a broad manner, and at that time a few restraints imposed beforehand may not be a bad thing. At least if one's commander has had the foresight to perceive some of the problems one will be facing.

All that day on the *Vulture* we remained uncertain as to what would happen. I was fairly sure Arnold would turn up, though when, heaven perhaps knew. I am not usually a great worrier, but when there is something like this in front of me, a single task I have to perform which depends just about entirely on the cooperation of another person, then I am anxious. It was hard to put one's mind on anything else, although I tried. Robinson was not a great deal of help. I was sitting on the quarterdeck sketching the hilly flanks of Hudson's river, and he kept coming up from the wardroom. "No sign of him yet?" or "Where has the damned fellow got to?" He would go and stand at the taffrail for a few minutes, looking upstream, and then stamp below decks again. Have you read the Reverend Gilpin on the delights of the picturesque? Well, they were all here, on the river in September light; if I'd had some watercolours I would have tried to catch their tints as well as their outline. In the late afternoon, a golden glow. And yet even the delights of landscape are not sufficient, especially when one's attention yearns for an object to appear suddenly in the frame of one's vision, a speck which becomes a barge, a mast, a flag fluttering, a flicker of movement which is seen to be the oars moving on each side as the barge approaches and each person in it becomes distinct. But no barge came. I let my mind drift to what I had left behind in the city—or should I say the town? Perhaps Sutherland was right about where our real interests lay! I have a satirical poem, a lengthy piece of doggerel is what it is, which is appearing in sections in *Rivington's* gazette. The subject of the piece is that excursion in Jersey, in which your General Wayne—Mad Anthony—figured so prominently. I had hoped to see the final canto into the press. Printers have a way of making their own contributions and emendations, which aren't always what one wants. We had also hoped to start rehearsals for a production of *The*

Beaux' Stratagem late next month. And—a final worry
—I was nervous at leaving Sir Henry too long alone.
He has a fatal urge to quarrel with other senior officers,
and this is something that I and a few other aides have
devised ways of circumventing. He feels that Whitehall has left it entirely up to him to make the best of a
bad job; he believes that he isn't given the support he
requires. He may be right.

That evening it was faro instead of whist. Since
Lord North imposed a tax on cards and dice, I suppose
you could say that we were contributing to the
finances of the war. For such an old ramrod, Sutherland was skillful or lucky at cards, and he took several
shillings off me and Robinson. He said that he planned
to move the *Vulture* downriver next morning if no
one had showed up by then; he thought that we were
flaunting the British presence here, and were liable to
attack. It was getting on for midnight when I decided
to turn in, and I was just doing so when word was
brought down that a barge had come alongside. For
an instant I felt upset and disappointed. I had come
round to thinking that nothing would happen, and
that this would be just as well. So for the moment I
was not relieved! And in the event our visitor was not
the enterprising Major General; he had sent an emissary in his place.

He was waiting in the wardroom when Robinson
and I—in shirt and waistcoat—returned there.
(Sutherland refused to reappear.) "Mr. Joshua Hett
Smith," said the young officer of the watch who was
with him, and Mr. Smith got to his feet, a stocky,
middle-aged man with a rather cautious look to him—
perhaps simply from the fact that he had never been
on board a ship before. I recognized in him some of

the features of his older brother, as I presumed him to be, William, our Chief Justice in New York. He seemed to know Robinson, who introduced me as Mr. John Anderson. Their conversation made clear that Smith was a landowner on the west side of Hudson's, and after a few pleasantries about the weather and the harvest, Smith reached into a deep side pocket and drew forth a sheaf of papers, which he handed to Robinson. I poured Mr. Smith a glass of madeira, while Robinson first perused them and then handed them to me. They were: an open letter from Arnold to Robinson, mentioning proposed commercial transactions between them; a pass, signed by Major General Arnold, permitting Joshua Smith, Esquire, to go to Dobb's Ferry with three men and a boy to carry letters of a private nature for gentlemen in New York; a second pass, also signed by General Arnold, giving permission to "Joshua Smith, Esq., a gentleman Mr. John Anderson, who is with him, and his two servants to pass and repass the guards near King's Ferry at all times"; and a final fragment of paper, which Robinson handed to me with a conclusive grunt, and which had four words penned on it—*Gustavus to John Anderson*. It was a scrap small enough to swallow or tread into the bilges of a boat.

Beverley Robinson addressed Smith: "Tell me, sir, when did you last see General Arnold?"

"He has been at my house since sunset. We had some trouble acquiring men to row the barge out here."

"These papers indicate that it is you—and Mr. Anderson here—who will be doing the travelling. Did General Arnold give you his reasons for not joining us here himself?"

"No, he did not. He asked me to bring Mr. Anderson ashore."

"I am not convinced that such a course is best, or necessarily safe for Mr. Anderson."

"It will be on neutral ground, Colonel," said Smith. His eyes glanced up for a moment at the low overhead of the wardroom ceiling, as if he thought it might be he who was not safe in these nautical confines. "The General proposes to be at the Old Trough, near Long Clove, about one o'clock. The road comes close to the river there—though it means climbing a steep bank to reach it. It's not far from de Noyelle's," he added, as though Robinson's former residence on the other side of the river would qualify him to recognize these names and landmarks.

"How long will it take to row in?" I asked. I felt Robinson look at me as if he wanted to kick my shin for showing any enthusiasm for the proposed plan.

"Twenty minutes, more or less," Mr. Smith said. "There are a number of American guard boats out on the river—but we have the password of the night, if we are stopped."

"I was about to say," Robinson interjected, "what do you intend to do if you are stopped?"

"We say 'Congress,' " said Smith. "And we present General Arnold's pass if necessary."

"I still don't favour it," said Robinson. "He should come out to us."

Smith did not reply to this; perhaps he felt that it had nothing to do with him, the decisions that were taken; he was merely acting as a messenger in regard to matters of a "private nature." Or if he did know more, he did not intend to show it. Certainly anyone might regard as curious a senior American officer visiting a British sloop-of-war in the middle of the night, however personal the transactions were purported to be.

"If Mr. Anderson is to go ashore, then I should accompany him," Robinson said.

I pointed out that although the open letter was addressed to him, the passes did not mention him, only me. My eagerness, combined with what was I think no great enthusiasm on his part to go ashore, served its purpose. I asked Mr. Smith if he would mind waiting on deck while I had a final word with Colonel Robinson. Smith went out, bidding a courteous good night to Robinson and saying to me, "We should make haste. It will take time . . ." I waved him on; I would follow soon, I said.

"You're determined, then?" said Robinson. "I could wish the situation were a little, well, sharper. This Joshua Smith, for instance. Where does he stand? Can we really rely on him?"

"Arnold has trusted him with this. For the rest, does it matter? I should be back before dawn, with any luck. So much hangs on this meeting. It would be foolish to withdraw now."

We shook hands. Robinson wished me Godspeed. As I went into my little cabin to collect my coat and cape, I could hear Sutherland snoring next door. Then, seeing Robinson still at the foot of the companionway, I asked him to look after one of my two watches—the silver one my mother had given me on the twenty-first anniversary of my birth, inscribed *Cher Jean*. I kept the gold hunter.

I see, Tallmadge, you have two men posted in the garden. Is this in case I choose to dive through the window? Perhaps you will permit me a well-guarded stroll out there in a while. This room feels like a ship's cabin and I would welcome a turn on deck. I doubt if I will plunge overboard—at least not yet. I wonder whether you have ever felt as I did, as I stepped from the waist of the *Vulture*, climbed over the bulwarks and down the ladder into Smith's barge. The *Vulture* lay towards New York, into the tide, and the moving water pushed between ship and boat with a noisy gurgle. Noisy enough, I thought, to cover any rumbles in my stomach. I have never ceased to suffer from stagefright, and as I stepped into the boat, as it rocked a little with my weight, it was as if the curtains were about to draw apart.

There were only two oarsmen, which seemed little for the heavy open barge. The water was dark and, once away from the *Vulture*'s side, without a ripple. I sat in the bows and watched the black silhouette of the ship slowly merge with the blackness of the shore behind. No moon, no stars. I pulled the blue watch cape close over my chest, covering my uniform jacket. The men were grumpy-looking devils, from what I could see of them as they pulled at their oars. The only sounds were the splash and plop as the blades dipped in and came out again and the barge crabbed slowly across the river. Smith, in the stern sheets, directed a course that seemed to allow something for the tide. I tried to compose my mind, as before a play, for the part I was taking. It was a matter of throwing into a melting pot different proportions of artifice and reality, and hoping that the resulting concoction was convincing. I am John Anderson, I told myself, a British gentleman on a personal errand dealing with a private commercial matter. What that matter was, as in many such transactions, naturally had to be kept confidential. But it was hard to keep my mind set only on this. I thought of other journeys in small boats. In Geneva, on the lake, with my father, rowing along the shore one evening toward Morges, with Mont Blanc just visible to the south like a giant angel spreading out its white wings. And in Philadelphia, during our farewell celebrations for our commander Sir William Howe, I was one of those in charge—it made a change from usual staff duties—and arranged a nighttime procession of galleys and barges on the river there. Flaming torches lit the way. We were in medieval costume as knights and ladies. I had agreed to accompany Margaret Chew a few days before I met Margaret Shippen. The two Peggies. Of course, there had been no turning back; no way of saying, "I think I have fallen in love with your friend and would rather escort her."

"Stop rowing!" Smith's whisper was as loud as a whisper can be. The barge quickly lost way. We listened. It was easy to imagine things. Yet there came a real sound—a man's laugh, upriver from us. Smith put the tiller over and said softly, "Row briskly." He said to me, "Did I mention it before? The watchword if we are stopped is 'Congress.'" He *had* mentioned it, and why I needed to be reminded, I don't know—was he going to be too rattled to speak? If Congress could have seen us! All those speechifying Rebels who had held up Arnold's promotion and were so persistent in questioning his accounts!

Slowly the height of the dark wall ahead of us increased. The oars swung reluctantly back and forth. Then the cliff loomed overhead. I could hear the water lapping against the stones along the shore.

"There's one spot where we can land easily," mur-

mured Smith. "A small point, with a single tree on it."
We rowed slowly along the shore for five minutes or
so.

"A devil of a way to earn fifty pounds of flour,"
muttered one of the oarsmen.

"Aye, Sam, it is."

I thought disagreeably that at this rate we would
still be rowing up and down the river with dawn
breaking. Was Arnold in fact waiting on the bank
above? I thought I could hear a horse whinnying up
there. I suggested to Smith that we row as close to the
shore as possible, in order to be able to see the lone tree
on the point against the somewhat lighter river and
sky. Smith said, "There are rocks to think about." But
he took the barge in closer, and within a minute we
glimpsed the outline of a tree. A small spit of land.
There was the suggestion of a beach, a few yards at
least of landing place. The bows of the barge crunched
on shingle and sand. On the bank above, the noise of
movement, the snap of twigs, and the rustle of bending
branches. I stepped ashore.

Tallmadge, my dear man, isn't it time you took the
weight off your feet? Perhaps you want Lieutenant
King to relieve you for a while? Anyway, be seated. I
too shall put my feet up, and a little later, when the
afternoon sun makes its appearance, I shall draw. Draw
rather than write. I fear the Muse of amorous and
satiric verse may have abandoned me for good, a lost
cause. I would be interested to know how General
Arnold struck you, but your views would no doubt be
influenced by what you know now, apart from your
conceptions as a patriot and a partisan. My idea of him,
prior to our meeting, was tinged by two feelings. The

first was envy. Peggy Shippen was a delectable creature, young as she was, the vital flame of the little society of Third and Fourth Streets in Philadelphia. She could have chosen from half a dozen of my fellow officers when we were in occupation there. But however devoted to her we became—and I was not the only one to be drawn to her—and however flatteringly flirtatious she was, there was always a feeling that, for example when dancing with one of us, she was looking around for her next capture. Not that we expected her to go after a man nearly twice her age, from the other side. I suppose we should congratulate her on her powers of perception, since she must have realized that he was not altogether on your side—indeed, was on no side at all, perhaps, at that moment, other than his own. I don't mean to sound bitter; it is the bitterness of hindsight. And please don't imagine that Peggy was part of a deep plot dreamed up by me to suborn Arnold's loyalties. Maybe that occurred to her later, once she had married him. I think your rebellion may not have seemed to her quite the right thing.

The second feeling that influenced my opinion of Arnold was straightforward admiration of his behaviour in action. From what I had heard, nearly every engagement he had participated in had been positively affected by his decisiveness. There was his march up the Kennebec River to attack Quebec; his actions on Lake Champlain; his role at Saratoga. It has often seemed that our commanders on both sides have gone out of their way to avoid committing themselves to a great battle. Arnold is an exception. He seeks conflict. That quality made him a prize worth gaining, as Sir Henry himself understood. The fact that he remained in General Washington's favour, despite his financial troubles in Philadelphia, was of course also to his advantage.

I suppose I should add a third feeling, which was registered on the debit side of Arnold's account in my mind. He was a disgruntled man. All soldiers complain, I know; it is the military nature. But they let their dissatisfaction out, they complain to one another. It is the disgruntlement that lies deep that makes a man uncertain, even to himself. (Sir Henry may be another case in point.) You must understand, then, that I knew more or less what I was getting into.

And yet, Tallmadge, isn't it generally true that we can set aside doubts and difficulties in regard to other people's involvement in a venture if we feel that a successful outcome will enhance our own fortunes? I sought a commission originally to do just that. My father had me in mind to succeed him in his merchant's business, but I lasted only a year in the countinghouse. I had seen Geneva. I knew there was a world beyond Hackney, with its tidy villas, and beyond the City, with its ledgers and bills. And I had also seen Lichfield, with its fine houses set around the cathedral close. I had ridden slowly past the gates of country estates. I knew that there were things to be achieved that in my case only the army offered a means to—unless one turned Macheath and made a fortune robbing coaches. So that is part of my impulse. And another part is that I wanted to demonstrate to Sir Henry, and of course to myself, that I was capable of more than diligent paperwork, of more than being amiable and charming. I could act—I could cause things to happen. A word I can mention now, to you, that I would probably not have dared breathe in New York among my friends is "glory." What I wanted was of that order, a prolonged form of the applause that greets the actor when his performance is a success. To be talked of in the army, rewarded by the King, recorded in the pages of history. Something that would last a little longer than the petty pleasures and pains of life. What else is worth fighting for?

I hope this apple is not all you are allowing me for a midday repast. How red it is! Scarlet coats, they hide the blood, they attract a woman's eye. Why are your trees redder than ours, Tallmadge, at this time of year? I say *your* trees to preserve the distinction of sides between us, though, in truth, after six long years on these shores, I feel that they are my trees, too. What are our differences?

Smith had vanished up the cliff into the trees and darkness, but after several minutes he appeared again with a slither and a bump. "The General is here," he said. He turned to the oarsmen and told them to remain there with the barge. He said to me, "It's not far. There's something of a path."

If so, I did not see it. Smith may not have looked like much of a woodsman, but he ascended the cliff once more with little fuss, certainly with the advantage of having done it before. I hauled myself up the bank after him, hanging on to branches, my feet planted askew in a little ditch that had been worn by rain in the root-tangled soil. I ran into boughs and had to push them down or aside. Then there was loose shale underfoot and a strong smell roundabout of damp vegetation, of rotten wood and wet leaves. I imagined that there was also the poisonous American ivy, but it was too dark to tell. Smith, ahead of me, was waiting for me on a ledge where, in an opening of the trees and brush, the widened track slanted up the hill. Two shapes that became evident as horses stood under the trees, quite still. There were two other figures—one lying on the ground, apparently asleep, near the horses. The other came towards me, dipping to one side with a limp. He put his face close to mine and gave me a long, unblinking stare.

"It's Anderson, is it?"

"Yes."

"You're late. What detained you?"

Smith said: "There was difficulty with the boatmen. Then we had the tide against us much of the way to the ship."

"Come this way," Arnold said to me, as if meaning to waste no more time. "There's a flat dry spot where we can sit."

I refer to him as Arnold, although he had shown me no proof of his identity; I had intended to ask for some; it was, after all, a purpose of this meeting, to assure Sir Henry that my correspondence had been with Arnold himself. But now that I was here and in this man's presence, I had no doubt as to who he was. He had a conviction about himself which was communicated to me even in the darkness. I followed him a little way to the place he had chosen. Smith said quietly that he would wait below. The groom with the horses remained stretched out.

The night haze which had blanketed the river was removed from up here. Stars appeared through a wide gap in the foliage overhead, and the faint light made it possible, as my eyes became accustomed to the spot, to distinguish my companion's features: longish nose, heavy cheeks, a thickset, even burly, physique. The hair was black, the eyes deeply dark, though at moments a hard, diamondlike glitter was reflected from them. He began to speak again in the same impatient tone he had used before. "Well, we don't have to use Blackstone on this occasion. I'm pleased that we have met at last. Mrs. Arnold has spoken of you. Let us proceed to business."

There was no apology for not having turned up ten days before at Dobb's Ferry. No reference to the stratagem I had adopted of countersigning the complaint about the rebel fire upon our flag of truce, by which I had let him know that I was aboard the *Vulture*. No explanation as to why he had not come to the *Vulture* but had caused me to be brought ashore to meet him. He said: "Have you brought any of the money with you?"

That was forthright enough! No fencing around. I had a sudden memory of *The Recruiting Officer*, Farquhar's comedy—now I was the recruiting officer, and the recruit was a major general discussing his terms of engagement. I said at once that I had not brought any of the reward with me, nor was it on the *Vulture*. Sir Henry Clinton would be gratified to present it in person, with his congratulations, in New York. It would be, as our correspondence had indicated, twenty thousand pounds for the successful capture by us of West Point and its outposts, together with all stores, arms, and ammunition. We confidently expected to seize upwards of three thousand troops. In regard to rank, the seniority of other serving officers had to be considered, but the Major General would receive in our army the substantive rank of colonel, the acting rank of brigadier, and a command which would soon lead one of his ability to higher military honours. There would also be an annuity of five hundred pounds a year. If our plans went awry, which we did not expect but must consider, and if General Arnold was forced to take refuge at New York, then an indemnity of six thousand pounds would be paid, with all other perquisites of rank, commands and pensions remaining the same.

This did not satisfy him. I had been conscious of speaking in a deliberately low voice, for we were close together, seated on our cloaks spread upon the slanting ground; he spoke firmly, as if we had been strolling around the same parade ground together at midday. He said he was taking a large risk. He had a young wife, a new child. There was a great amount that he would have to leave behind if (as he also did not expect) our plans failed—the four years' pay that he was owed by Congress; a house in New Haven and another property in Philadelphia; money owed him by Connecticut for depreciation in pay; future benefits forfeited, such as land promised by Congress and some of the states. Six thousand would not begin to cover these expectations.

I had had a letter from him a few months earlier in which he had started this haggling. Ten thousand had been the sum he had named as the guarantee he wanted in the event of failure. But the risk of failure would surely be less if we didn't spend all night sitting and talking about money. The fate of a war swayed in the balance while petty bargaining went on. I told him that I could see the reasons for his arguments, but the figure my commander had allowed me to confirm was six thousand. I suggested that I would do my best to have the sum increased, in the event the plan did not succeed and General Arnold had to quit the American service, but that at that moment I could do no more than give him such an assurance. I reflected, but did not say, that it had been disagreements over money which had brought the Colonies and the mother country to the present pitch; the American objections to taxes such as the stamp duties imposed by Britain to defray the costs of defending these lands, which would not, after all, exist (unless as French possessions) if it had not been for the valour of British arms —with valuable Colonial assistance, to be sure.

Arnold was silent for a moment, too. It was as if he was fighting with his own touchiness (I had been told he had fought a duel with some Frenchman in the West Indies for the slightest of provocations). But perhaps he decided his own pride was best served on this occasion by dropping the subject. And once that aspect of things had been set aside, his determination and concentration fixed on purely military matters. Indeed, he spoke almost as if *I* had been the one keeping us from this! "We must move swiftly—and I am glad Sir Henry realizes it," he said. "Today is Friday the twenty-second. Washington will not return from his meeting with the French at Wethersfield before midday on Monday. I shall probably know exactly, because he will call at Robinson's House and West Point on his way to the camp at Tappan. You will be back in New York tomorrow, Saturday, at the latest. If Rodney's squadron is prepared, as you say it is, then it could sail upriver on Sunday. Let us allow twelve hours for forty miles. High tide Monday morning is about seven, a little later upriver. So it should be West Point just after dawn, Monday. Tuesday if wind and weather are unfavourable. You will have West Point, and—with good fortune—Washington, too."

He went on to describe the dispositions he had made

at West Point: where the men were stationed and where the best places for the assault would be. He had already dispersed his troops in a way that rendered the place less secure. He would send out further parties to cut firewood. When news of the British approach arrived from the posts at King's Ferry and Verplanck's, on the river between here and West Point, he would send out detachments into the Highland gorges, as though to meet the British forces, which would then be able to sail past and land safely and consolidate their positions behind the Rebels' backs. The American detachments at King's Ferry and Fishkill, above West Point on the east bank of the river, had standing orders to repair to West Point if it came under attack. But they would not get there in time, except to be captured.

I shifted my sitting position slightly. I felt through my cape the damp residual in the ground. The stars continued to look down through the gap in the trees. I said, "Could you tell me the condition of the various forts and redoubts at the Point?"

"I was just about to. Fort Putnam is a shambles—in great need of restoration. Its eastern wall is broken down. The wall on the west has numerous gaps. You will also need to know the locations of the bombproof stores and provision magazines."

When he had listed these, I asked for the numbers of men presently at West Point.

"I can see you are a diligent man, Mr. Anderson." In his voice there was a note of sardonic approval. "In the Point and dependencies, three thousand and eighty-six, by last week's count. But you will not have to remember all this. I have written it down. Together with notes on the forts, a table of ordnance, and artillery orders for September the fifth, wherein is described how the corps will be disposed in case of alarm. And the minutes of the Council of War at headquarters on September the sixth, at which the lack of provisions and funds were discussed. It should make encouraging reading for General Clinton."

I asked, "How are these written down?"

"A small roll of papers. It shouldn't trouble you to carry them back. You may tie a stone to them and, if you have to, throw them overboard."

He made no motion to hand me these papers. I wondered how to refuse them. Perhaps they were in a saddlebag on his horse, still standing quietly where it was tethered. I didn't need the papers. The Council of War minutes were not important. I have an excellent memory—plenty of practice as an actor!—and could repeat almost word for word what had been said about the fortifications and the disposition of troops. Sir Henry knew well the face of the land around West Point; he had reconnoitered there while in possession of the Highland forts. Papers could be a damned nuisance. Sir Henry had in his final instructions to me told me not to take any needless risks. I would be ill-advised, he said, to put off my uniform, to go within the American lines, or receive any papers. And here they were! Of course I knew that commanders now and then give instructions that protect themselves and their consciences if things go wrong, and if things don't go wrong you may well find yourself rebuked for not having shown independent resolution. Here, Arnold presumably wished me to take the papers to New York in order to demonstrate his allegiance, to show Sir Henry that the Crown was getting full value. And if anything untoward happened to Arnold during the attack, the papers would be evidence that he had done his job. A pension for Peggy.

On the hillside a bird let forth a solitary note. Although no others joined it, I wondered how long it would be before the dawn. Arnold was asking about the ships in Rodney's squadron—their armaments, the depth of water that they drew. He could recommend two, possibly three, places for landing the troops. The chain and boom that were stretched across the river from West Point to Constitution Island were in weakened condition, with many of their iron links in need of replacement. If we felt that we needed to land north of this, a frigate sailing full and bye with the flood current could easily sunder the chain. He described the main trails leading up to the Point and suggested which of them it would be best to follow. He listed places where assault parties could form up under good cover. He went over the terrain very nearly foot by foot, and as I listened to him I had the impression that he was already there on the morning of the engagement. He was in charge and was waving us forward.

He thought we should also arrange signals, to determine the surrender and for indicating his own position. But the night silence was now being resolutely broken. The hillside had awakened, and every bird on it seemed to be contributing to the overture before the dawn. Moreover, someone was coming up the path. Mr. Smith.

"General," he said, "it will soon be daybreak."

Arnold got to his feet; he lifted each leg in turn, bending it at the knee, to restore vitality to the limbs. He said, "Are the Cahoons set for the row back to the ship?"

"Well, that's just it. That's why I thought I had better disturb your talk. They won't row out again. They say they're too fatigued. By the time we set out back from the *Vulture*, the ebb and the river current would be against us all the way to Haverstraw—but there's a bit of flood left now to help from here. They're also worried about being stopped by the guard boats, with sunrise coming on."

"Those numbskulls," said Arnold furiously. "I've written passes. I'd better go down."

"General, I don't think it will help. You recall how difficult it was to get them to row out tonight. They're obstinate. They won't go again."

I was still sitting down, which was perhaps just as well. You know how it is when you are approaching a position you are certain is safe and suddenly a cannon shot whizzes past you—the air seems to explode, to push you aside. I felt dizzy. Perhaps it is like this in an earthquake or an avalanche. But together with the surprise, which upset me, I felt angry. What a stupid predicament! Here we were arranging plans with precise care and yet were in the hands of Smith and his damned Cahoons!

Arnold, however, scarcely paused; it was the work of an instant to rearrange this aspect of the scheme. He said, "Then Mr. Anderson will return with me to your house, Joshua. He can stay there during the day. We will send him back at nightfall."

"You don't think that—"

Arnold cut him short. "No. That's the way it will be." So I was not given the benefit of knowing what alternatives Smith had been going to suggest.

"I will get started, then," said Smith. "The barge must be returned to the creek."

September 28

"Take David with you. Then Mr. Anderson may ride his horse."

Smith roused the groom, whom I now saw to be a black man, and they went down the hillside. I listened to the branches bending and the shale sliding under their feet and wished that I were with them. Should I have insisted on going out, or at least on not riding to Smith's house with Arnold? Should I have said that I would remain there on the wooded hillside until it grew dark again, when they could collect me? I should have discussed with Robinson just such an eventuality. A boat from the *Vulture* could have been ready to come in for me at a signal. Too late now. The chance of refusing Arnold had slipped away, would have been awkward to retrieve. Perhaps the fourteen hours would not make a deal of difference. I would still be in New York on the morrow, in the *Vulture* or one of its boats. I trusted Robinson and Sutherland not to panic when I failed to return to them by daybreak.

We rode in silence. The track that led from where we had been sitting climbed the hillside, then dipped into a gully that ran at a right angle to the river, between the hills. This was the Short Clove, I assumed. We skirted the edge of what seemed to be a small quarry and then followed beneath the shoulder of a considerable hill, High Tor, I believe, which I had seen from the *Vulture*. The sky to the east was lightening. For the first time I could clearly see my broad-shouldered companion. He sat his horse easily, having mounted it in an agile way, with no hint of being hindered by his injured leg. I was riding a little behind, and for an instant this "hindsight" and the overhanging wooded slopes in the first morning light brought to my mind an engraving I'd seen somewhere of a highwayman. Since I was unseen, I allowed myself the comfort of a smile. Perhaps the term "privateer" was more appropriate. Part of me admired the man. It must be hard to change sides—it involves admitting that one has been wrong up until that moment; it means anticipating the wrath of one's friends. But I felt this whole venture would have been made easier if I had liked and trusted him.

Riding at a good pace, we soon came to the outskirts of a settlement. Perhaps too grand a name for a dozen wooden cottages strung alongside the road. We were still a little way off when I saw a man appear—he detached himself from the shadow of a house and thrust himself from a doorway out into the road, musket in one hand, pulling straight his shabby coat. It was a nervous snap of a voice that came out of him: "*Stand!*"

Arnold did not rein back his mount. "Major General Arnold and aide," he said as he moved by. " 'Congress.' "

"Yes, sir. Pass along, sir." The guard produced an exaggerated salute.

I clutched my cape tight around my regimental jacket—to hide it, though the movement also had the effect of constraining a feeling that I wanted to shiver violently. I felt cold, then hot, with fear and fury. I was compelled to wait awhile, until we had ridden past the village, before I spoke. "Then we are inside your lines."

"Yes. Belmont, Smith's house, is a mile or so north of here. This is Haverstraw."

Arnold seemed to assume that this topographical information would suffice; it was as if he supposed that I should have known that going to Smith's meant going behind the Continental lines. Yet I was now doing what I had explicitly refused to do when he had proposed by letter that I meet him at Robinson's House. I was doing what Sir Henry had clearly instructed me not to do. In fact, I *had* done it. And how was I to turn back? Only the blue watch cape covered the scarlet jacket that proclaimed me a British officer on American-held ground. The momentum of my errand seemed to be taking me further onto that ground. Arnold rode on, seemingly unconcerned. I felt the leather of the reins in my hands—a single tug would halt me here. We could thrash the matter out. I think if Arnold had shown the slightest hesitation, had manifested the least hint that he perceived I had reasons for being offended, I would have stopped for such a discussion. But he did not. It was left to me. And I believe that I was ashamed of showing what might be taken for fear. It is the only way that I can explain it. Circumstances formed such a web.

It was not long before we reached Belmont, on a cleared hillside. By then it was fully light. The house looked almost new, a two-storey stone building with a single-storey wing on each side. An imposing flight of steps led up to a porch with a centrally placed front door. I am susceptible to architecture. This house, constructed solidly, had pleasing proportions, and yet it did not charm me. There were no intimations of warm hospitality. I paused on the porch and looked back down the clearing over the lower woods. The river was visible, a wide, curving band of pink-grey, reflecting the sunlight like a sword, and to one side a few shingle roofs in Haverstraw.

"Come in," said Arnold, pushing open the door as if

he was at home here. "Come in—you must not be seen. Not that anyone's here right now. Smith's family are away. From upstairs you will be able to observe your ship."

He went ahead of me upstairs. He led me to a front room and opened its door with a "Here you are." I thought for a moment that he would now apologize for having brought me here, for the behaviour of the oarsmen, for the necessity of coming behind the American lines, but there was nothing of this sort, merely a remark to the effect that he was going to clean up before breakfasting, which he imagined we would in an hour or so, on Smith's return from the river. The room was a good deal larger than this one, Tallmadge. Much more genteelly furnished. A mahogany-framed bed. A fine embroidered counterpane. Desk with a silver inkstand. Elegant wallpaper. One had the impression that the Smiths had gone to the best suppliers, and perhaps that was the impression they wished to make. I took off my cape and jacket and considered the bed. Although I was tired, I did not feel sleepy—I was too jumpy and irritated to be able to sleep. I pulled the muslin curtains aside at the window, opened the top sash to let in the air, and looked out over the hillside, the village, the river, and beyond the river to the east the rugged landscape that stretched away, pale green at that time of day. Hessian Hill. Spitzenberg Mountain. It was strange to feel moved by that prospect even in the disagreeable situation in which I found myself. There was nothing of the trim, cultivated order of English countryside. Instead, what great sweeps, what expanses of colour! A panorama rather than a landscape, still waiting for man to shape it and derive sustenance from it. As yet unruled, however hotly fought over.

The *Vulture* from this distance looked like a toy. As a child I had had a miniature brig that I sailed on Lake Leman, at first on a long piece of hemp, but one day when the wind seemed to be steady I let it sail untethered. After giving it a push, I ran around to the other side of the little semicircular bay to wait for it to arrive at that shore. My brig was called *L'Espérance*. The wind changed. My brig was brought aback; then it wore around and sailed out of the bay into the lake. I watched it until I could no longer see it—though I believed I could still make out its topsail long after it must have disappeared. I came back every day for some time, thinking it might have sailed back to its harbour. *L'Espérance!* As for the *Vulture*, she rode at anchor just north of Teller's Point, where I had left her. It seemed bizarre, jarringly out of kilter, that I could see them, indeed almost imagine what Robinson was doing, whereas those on board had lost sight of me completely. I was as enveloped in these woods as a swimmer would be who had fallen overboard while on passage to this continent and was immersed in the immense sea. I imagined myself standing on the *Vulture*'s quarterdeck, peering through one of the ship's leather-covered telescopes at the hillside above Haverstraw: a speck of a house, an upstairs window, the minute figure of a man looking out . . . Could I will myself aboard?

Now the sun rose, orange and fat, over the hills to the east. It was neither busy nor unruly today—one would need to be otherwise, perhaps amorously, preoccupied, to abuse it thus. It was simply on time, according to the almanacs and my pocket hunter; it was just six. And with it there came abruptly the sound of gunfire—several salvos. Howitzer and cannon.

For an instant I thought that the firing sounds came from New York, carried by some freak of air this far upriver. Today was the anniversary of His Majesty's Accession. Salutes of twenty-one guns would be fired from Fort George and the ships in the harbour. Was this the *Vulture* firing a salute? But I reflected that not even a punctilious sense of protocol would cause Sutherland to do anything so ridiculous right there. Furthermore, any salutes in town would be fired at one in the afternoon. I could now see gunsmoke rising from Teller's Point. The sounds of firing came across the river in a regular sequence. And small puffs of grey smoke appeared around the *Vulture*. Fire was being returned.

"It's Livingston." Arnold was standing beside me, cold with anger. "He asked me two days ago for heavier cannon. I put him off. I didn't want him engaging your ships as they came upriver. He seems to have had a four-pounder dragged down from Verplanck's to Teller's. Very eager is Livingston."

In the nearby treetops birds were chirruping. Two and a half miles away cannonball and grapeshot were being exchanged. It seemed unreal, a toy battle. Why didn't the *Vulture* get under way? I watched for the flutter of sails being unloosed from the yards. Of course, it was too calm; the treetops didn't stir. Boats, then—boats to warp her along out of range. Get going! But no, they appeared to wish to stay and fight it out. Arnold said that if he were captain of the

Vulture, he would send a landing party to sort the villains out.

The little engagement went on for nearly an hour. It was well past seven when the *Vulture* weighed anchor, her canvas hanging limp, and drifted out into midstream and slowly downriver. She was pursued by a final splash in the widening stretch of water between her and Teller's Point. And just as she passed from sight, obscured from my vision by trees on the hillside below Belmont, the sound of a large explosion came from the Point. A tall plume of smoke ascended. It was like the last grand piece of a fireworks display.

"I don't think that was the sloop's doing," Arnold said. "I believe their powder store has blown up."

Well, it would have been better blowing up an hour before. It would have been better had I got back to the ship before dawn. It would . . . I recalled the toy brig which had never come back from its independent voyage on the lake. I knew Sutherland and Robinson would do all they could to avoid abandoning me, but circumstances might compel them to.

Isn't it time we had a change of mood, Major Tallmadge? I should hope we will dine soon. Meanwhile, I'll see what fancies I can summon up to divert us. In moments like this it would be pleasant to have Prospero's powers, to conjure Ariel or even Caliban. For all his foul shape, the child of Sycorax has many of the sweetest lines to say. As Prospero I could magic myself out of here, I suppose, well away from Tappan's trepidations—or will it be trepanations? You see how insistent these worries are. I must make more of an effort to shake them off. Let's not talk of graves and worms and epitaphs. When were you last in love, Tallmadge? Or when were you first in love? That may be easier to answer.

It may encourage you if I make my confessions first. Her name was—is—Honora. I was eighteen when we met. Seven years later, at the time I was taken prisoner at St. John's, I was stripped of all my possessions by your soldiers. They took everything except a locket containing a portrait of Honora, which I concealed in my mouth. So you can see, the affliction lasted. It was a miniature I had drawn of her, one of two. I gave her the other. It had also kept me going during my countinghouse days. I would allow myself a glimpse of it when I reached the bottom of each page of a ledger. Honora called me Jean—*Cher Jean*. I had accompanied my mother from Clapton to the spa at Buxton, where she took the waters. Honora's father was there for his gout. Honora and I met in the assembly rooms. We were introduced, we drank tea and punch, we danced. I think dancing tells one a great deal about one's sympathies with another person, what in French is called *rapport*, the anticipation and response of one to another, sometimes while moving, turning, at dizzying speed. How we danced! But Mr. Sneyd—her mother was dead—was not particularly encouraging to the attentions I paid his daughter. You might have thought that a stripling like me would be conceded his possibilities and ambitions, rather than being condemned for his comparative poverty and lack of immediate prospects. On his wife's death Mr. Sneyd had distributed his five daughters among his friends, and Honora lived with Canon Seward and his family in the Bishop's Palace at Lichfield; but her papa retained a loving interest, and undoubtedly considered his Honora a worthwhile match for the heir to a thousand acres and at least five thousand sterling. Honora's closest friend was one of the two Seward sisters, Anna, and it was through her that we used to correspond. We were not allowed to write to each other directly. Miss Seward collected and forwarded our letters. And whenever I could, I used to take a chaise up there—one hundred and twenty bone-shaking miles, and worth every moment of discomfort on the way.

Lichfield is one of those English country towns that seem especially favoured: the calm cathedral close, the tall spires that can be seen from far out in the prosperous countryside. The sort of place where there are a surprising number of talented people. Both Johnson and Garrick—you have no doubt heard their names—are Lichfield men. Miss Seward had a coterie of such people around her, and she encouraged my drawing, my verse, and my interest in Honora. We used to meet in Miss Seward's dressing room, the blue region we called it, for it had blue velvet curtains, and blue Delft tiles around the fireplace—and Miss Seward was the friendliest of bluestockings. Honora and I talked about our parents' fondness for places like Buxton and Bath, which we both declared we found tedious. Too many plain women, I said. Too many dull men, said she. We excluded ourselves, of course, in this ungenerous assessment, and ignored the fact that Buxton had brought us together and allowed us to dance. We talked about the qualities of landscape that make it beautiful and about our aspirations, and we condemned the striving, mercenary, rank-conscious world. Rank and place, estate and income—fie and be damned with it! We were eighteen and revolutionaries!

Apart from when we were dancing, I must have touched her hand a dozen times, and our lips met twice. Once on the stairs, when Miss Seward had preceded us. Once in the cloisters, as we were going to evensong. Ours was an attraction enhanced by difficulty and distance—it was built up through correspondence, and each letter was like a supporting column in its structure. In her letters to me, she told me about her father's admonitions, and how the Canon and Mrs. Seward were attempting to divert her interests—French lessons were proposed, and piano practice had been intensified. I contrasted Clapton to Lichfield and the pleasant Vale of Stowe. I was writing from the midst of account books, of bills and other implements of gain. I used to pen the most extravagant fancies. Once, I remember, I regretted that language did not offer up my feelings freshly enough, that whatever one communicated by letter had to go in such a roundabout way before it reached one's correspondent. It had to travel from the writer's heart through his head, arm, hand, pen, ink, and paper, and then over many a weary hill and dale, to the eye, head, and heart of the reader. If only we possessed a faculty that enabled our sensations and remarks to rise from their source in a sort of exhalation and fall upon the paper in words and phrases suited to them—without having to pass through an imagination that so often failed to operate in proper support of the heart.

In fact, the zephyrs I was subject to were those wafting through the cracks in the countinghouse wainscot; my small coal fire created a draught which took all the heat in the room up the chimney. I felt most miserably that I would never be more than I was then. It was because of Honora that I wished for wealth and fame, that I dreamed of sumptuous palaces, or so I thought. I was reading Rousseau, and quoting him to Honora—"There are moments worth ages," trusting that she would understand what moments I referred to. But Honora's father and guardians were prepared for a longer siege than I. Obstacles were hinted at rather than threatened. The projected alliance of Miss Sneyd with Mr. André was thought unfortunate: it was throwing away her chances of far more influential and affluent connections. What were Mr. André's hopes and his talents compared to his lack of fortune? He was indeed a very bright and lively young man. But something steadier, more earnest, even less witty and charming, might have produced a more reliable impression.

Honora was not robust enough to withstand the Sneyd and senior Seward opposition. It seemed that Anna, too, was able to put to one side her romantic sympathy with the young pair and see it in more worldly terms; in other words, the attachment was delicious but imprudent, inspiring but incautious, so youthful in its enthusiasm but unrealistic in its ignorance of social necessity. Perhaps even she ceased to be the supporter we had counted on. On my last visit to Lichfield, Honora had a fever and Anna used this as an excuse why we should not see each other.

And so, when it came to it, the endless age in the André countinghouse did not seem worth it. Our characters matured and grew apart. I acquired my commission in '71. *Cher Jean* then seeks new fields to conquer. Honora, from half a dozen suitors favoured by the Canon and Mrs. Seward and Mr. Sneyd, chooses one Edgeworth, an ingenious man and a widower with at least one child. In the next act, young John André is posted to the New World. He is sufficiently ruthless or uninspired on one occasion to write to Miss Shippen in Philadelphia a poem which he had previously penned to Miss Sneyd in Lichfield. *Return, enraptur'd hours, when Delia's heart was mine, when she with wreaths of flowers my temples wou'd entwine* . . . And yet I have never ceased to think of Honora, particularly in these past days. *Now nightly round my bed no airy visions play, no flowers crown my head each vernal holiday. For far from these sad plains my lovely Delia flies, and rack'd with jealous pains, her wretched lover dies.*

I hope there is going to be nothing prophetic about that bit of verse, as a penalty for having employed it twice. Thank God, it is time to eat.

We breakfasted at Belmont in a somewhat strained atmosphere. It would have helped if I had known how much Arnold had taken Joshua Hett Smith into his confidence. The pretense, if pretense it was, was scarcely at all. Smith made urbane apologies for the plainness of the repast—bread, cheese, porter. His family and servants were up at Fishkill, visiting friends for a few days. He was supposed to go up so as to accompany them on their way home today or tomorrow. For his last guests, his household had managed to provide more enterprising fare. While he spoke, his gaze was fastened on my regimental coat, which I realized he was now seeing for the first time.

"Mr. Smith has been a busy host," Arnold explained. "First, Mrs. Arnold stayed here overnight on her way to Robinson's from Philadelphia. Then General Washington was here to dinner."

"He ate as if he hadn't seen food for several days,"

said Smith. "If the commander is hungry, the men must be on slim pickings." He gave a nervous laugh, perhaps wondering what would happen if either commander or men entered at that moment and saw a man in British uniform seated at his breakfast table.

"This is September," Arnold said. "What will it be like in January? In any event, my wife was highly pleased with the welcome here." He turned to me again. "The journey took seven days. She had our child with her."

I had heard from our correspondents in Philadelphia about this intended excursion and had been puzzled by its timing. Why at this moment had Arnold decided to bring Peggy to him? Surely it would restrict his movements and place her at least on the periphery of danger. Even if the attack on West Point were speedily and unbloodily concluded, the situation of a wife and infant at Robinson's would be bound to give rise to anxiety. Had I been in his shoes, I would have left her and the babe in Philadelphia with her parents. This admittedly might expose her to the chance of reprisals after the event, and the Philadelphia Council might be so aggravated by Arnold's defection that they took her hostage. But it would be safer. On the other hand, I realized these considerations could be ill based in that I had not seen the young woman in question for a year and six months. Perhaps it was Peggy herself who had insisted on joining her husband. Perhaps the Major General was so besotted with his pretty bride that he insisted she come to him, and she willingly did so. I remembered her as a great tease, the sort of girl who would get within an inch of you, eyes twinkling, hair shining, all fragrance—and then spin on her heels away once she saw that you were entranced. It would be a mistake to underestimate her cleverness, however lacking in years she might be. Perhaps she had seen in Arnold a maturity and forthrightness that had appeared wanting in us younger men, and perhaps, too, she had glimpsed the possibility of becoming in several swift moves a general's wife—a British general's wife.

Arnold seemed to realize that I was still thinking of her. "You'd better tell Colonel Robinson that she has rearranged his furniture," he said. There was a hint of smugness, of condescension—Peggy was *his*. The possessor spoke to those to whom he was prepared to grant in this way a vicarious enjoyment of his spirited young wife.

"You know Philadelphia, Mr. Anderson?" asked Smith, cutting into a further speculation I was making: Perhaps Arnold had considered that having Peggy close at hand furnished a very good cloak for his intentions.

I turned to Smith. "I was in business in Philadelphia for a year." A truthful reply, so far as it went. "I came over from London not long before the troubles began. My interests are now largely in New York." Also true. And it might remind Smith of the town I hoped to get back to as soon as possible. I wondered where the *Vulture* was now.

Arnold did not seem to like the drift of conversation. He said, "I should be getting back to headquarters. Mr. Anderson, pray come upstairs and we'll quickly address our transaction once more by daylight." He paused, deliberated. Then: "I shall have to leave it to Joshua to see you back tonight, one way or another."

"Your pardon, sir," I said. "I don't take your meaning."

There was a flash in his eyes at being thus called to

account, but the reply was put civilly enough, as if acknowledging the tremor of concern that had shivered through me. "I mean this. Naturally we hope that the *Vulture* will come back within reach. No doubt it will be preferred if we can convey you to her by boat. But—it may not be possible. We should allow for the fact that another route may be necessary."

"I don't desire it."

"I understand that. However—"

I broke in. "I left the *Vulture* in the strict belief that I would be returned to her directly."

"Of course. But this action of Livingston's has brought complications."

"I'm certain that the *Vulture* will not withdraw very far downriver." I wasn't absolutely certain; on the other hand, I was angry, and that showed—not that it moved Arnold.

"That may be," he replied. "However, as you well know, the exigencies of military action demand that we be prepared with alternative plans. In the event, the sloop may be impossible to reach. Joshua, would it be in order for you to ride with Mr. Anderson, say by way of King's Ferry, to the White Plains?"

"Yes, General."

It was clear to me that Arnold had had an alternative plan well prepared. I did not like it. I said, "My return would be quicker, easier, and safer on the river."

"I understand," Arnold said. "You will go that way if it can be managed."

It had reached a point where it was hard to reply without sounding petulant or fearful. Moreover, Arnold was not an enemy; he was my senior officer; we were both behind rebel lines. Presumably there were also difficulties in commanding Smith to do this or that. He was a civilian; he was apparently not privy to the plot; and impressing him with the urgency of getting me back might have the wrong effect, might cause him to lock solid as he had further reason to appreciate the perils of the venture in which he had become involved. So I nodded my head, as if accepting Arnold's reply, and as if my confidence that it would indeed turn out that way would help sway matters in that direction. To ride through the American lines would be entirely disagreeable and far more dangerous than returning by boat. If I went by land, there would be nothing for it but to get rid of my uniform and adopt a disguise.

Upstairs again, the uniform remained my concern; through talking about it, perhaps, I thought to convey my sense of aggravation with Arnold. I said, "How did you explain my regimentals to Mr. Smith?"

"I told him that you were a civilian who felt the need to impress—that you had borrowed the coat from a military acquaintance." He opened out on the bed a map of West Point and studied it; clearly he did not share the sense of horror I had at the prospect of being forced to dress as a civilian, and did not understand what disrespect it would be for my uniform to be worn by someone not entitled to wear it. Since we now had daylight and the map, he thought we should rehearse the attack once more, and refine our arrangements. He pointed out declivities, promontories, trails, and landing places. Trying to bring my full attention back to the matter, I proposed taking one wing of our forces up a certain track, but Arnold drew my notice to a ridge, which could be easily defended by a small number of the defenders, blocking the British way. A better route surely was by this path over here. And this was the place where I should look for the flag of surrender. Here was the spot where General Washington—if he had accepted the invitation to be there—would be presented to General Clinton.

I smiled at this, but Arnold's face was straight. Despite his remarks to me about needing to keep in mind alternative courses of action, he had no doubt about this, and certainly no doubts about his own role and its rectitude. His certainty seemed to lend firmness to the plan itself. It *would* succeed. Arnold said finally, "I will leave passes for you and Smith to show if you are stopped and questioned."

These were a necessity; I did not feel the need to express my obligation for them.

"And here," he went on, "are the papers for Sir Henry, with my compliments. As you see, Major, they're written out on very thin stuff. They'll fit in your stockings within your boots."

It was, I suppose, my chance to say that the papers were unnecessary—at least to *us*. Yet I understood his feelings that the papers, in Sir Henry's hands, bore witness to Arnold's loyalty to the British cause. They formed his *bona fides*. And the fact that he spoke and acted as a senior officer, referring to my rank, compounded the difficulty. I took them: a thin sheaf of papers.

"I count, then, on our meeting on Monday," Arnold said. He paused. I waited for him to shake my hand and wish me good luck. But he did neither; he said, "You'll remember our discussion about the guarantee? I hope for no less than ten thousand."

"Yes, General."

"Very well."

. . .

I watched him ride off with Smith down the hill. I assumed that Smith would accompany him to King's Ferry, where Arnold's barge would take him up to West Point. What would they be talking about on the way? It was just gone ten. I wound up my gold hunter. A breeze had begun to stir the branches of the trees nearest the house. Up high there were mare's tails. I wondered what some of our landscape improvers would have made of this prospect, with the marks of the frontiersman's axe still very nearly apparent. It had a rude nobility. And yet it was a long way from Lichfield. There, alongside the cathedral, ran a terraced walk bordered with flowering limes. "Good green people," Honora and I had called them. How horrified we were on finding that they were being lopped and stumpified on the orders of the reverend landlords, so that their tops made a straight line—more uniform than grenadiers on parade. But the limes would fight back, shooting out their boughs, performing their natural beaux stratagems. There was also a great willow in the garden of the Bishop's Palace, great yet sad in the way its boughs stooped to touch the ground. I used to enjoy the name Lichfield, a fine word to speak aloud, until Honora told me its old meaning. The field of dead bodies. The term "lich" as in lich gate, in a churchyard, where the coffin waits before interment. It seems that a number of Christian Britons had been massacred there by the Romans in Diocletian's time.

I laid down on the bed. It was going to be a long day of waiting. I closed my eyes. Spots of light, through my eyelids, circling. Sound of the muslin curtains swishing in the breeze that came through the window. It was a mildly ridiculous way for the acting adjutant

September 28

general of His Majesty's forces in New York to be spending an autumn day, virtually a prisoner in an empty house behind Continental lines. I had waited in vain for an apology from Arnold for recruiting me into this predicament. Merely: *au revoir* until Monday. I suppose that with his rank as commander in this area went a feeling of omnipotence. Oh, Anderson-André would get back to his chief, all right!

Joshua Hett Smith did not return all morning. I dozed from time to time, recouping a little of the sleep lost that night. The house was silent. At noon, awake, it occurred to me that in town soldiers would now be parading to mark the royal anniversary. Afterwards, my friends Beckwith and Delancey would repair to the King's Arms for a midday draught. The King, God bless him and save him! And then a toast to John André and success to his mission, whatever it may be. God bless him, too! But one trouble with thinking thus about jolly company when you are on your own is that it multiplies the feelings of loneliness. When I was a prisoner on parole in Lancaster, Pennsylvania, I used to spend much time in daydreams of an architectural or theatrical kind. I would design in my imagination stage sets and country houses, with no people inhabiting them, not even actors; but simply with glades and ruins, rooms and halls. I am of the school of Claude Lorrain when it comes to theatre landscape: dark trees in the foreground, sunlit vistas, enchanted palaces. And my country houses partake of the same desire for magical effect, for sunlight striking in through tall windows, while outside there are balustraded stone terraces, long avenues, a view across the lake, and then perhaps the merest glimpse of a party out riding or a woodcutter walking home. I suppose such thinking is harmless enough. Other men may ride to hounds in their head, make great speeches or sermons to imaginary crowds and congregations, or enjoy fantasies of wanton women. In my case, I sometimes planned the estate I would purchase if the investments that my father made shortly before his death eventually brought me a fortune—in fact, those investments, mostly in the West Indies, have fallen badly of late. On most such occasions the estate and landscape that I imagined was ideal and original to me. If you looked past the English fields and French woodland you might make out the snow-clad Alpine peaks. The manor was situated in my own country, which managed without Congress or King.

I must have dozed again. When I woke I could hear someone moving around on the floor below. I had been asked to stay out of sight, and I tried to quell my impatience to find out if Smith had returned and what arrangements he had made for restoring me to the *Vulture*. The front door slammed. There came the sound of a broom on the stone steps. From the window I could see the black head of the groom, presumably making things tidy for the return of Smith and his family. Last night I had thought he was Arnold's servant, but apparently he had been lent by Smith to the General to look after his horse. David. He swept with an economical motion, no abrupt whisks or flicks, simply back and forth, covering the area methodically, moving slowly on. I wondered about sounding him out. Many Negroes were Tory in sympathy. There was a blockhouse below Dobb's Ferry that was garrisoned by a gang of fugitive slaves, their strong-minded commander nicknamed Colonel Cuff. Their former masters hadn't considered them worthy of participation in the fight against Great Britain. I had heard that many blacks thought the King's armies were helping them by harassing the Colonists, by keeping the white Americans too busy to bother their black servants. Should I talk to him? He might know his way through the woods to the river's edge—might know where to lay his hands on a small boat. And yet, how did one talk to someone like that, how ask his help? Would I know where to begin?

It was a question of how ready I was to step outside the conventions. And, as I look back, it seems stupid of me not to realize that I was, willy-nilly, outside them already, through no single fault of my own. I could go down and try to talk to David, or I could continue to presume that Smith would do the job entrusted to him. After all, Arnold's success and safety were bound up with my own. He could hardly leave me in the lurch when his future depended on my reaching New York with our agreed plans. On the other hand, it was still a question whether Arnold had dared to convey to Smith how important my errand was. It was a question, and a flaw.

I dithered. At last I decided to go and speak to David. I went down the stairs whistling, to let him know of my presence. I would say that I needed to get to the river and the ship as soon as possible, and propose a reward if he helped me. But when I reached the front door, he was no longer there on the steps. I opened the door slightly to listen and look, and thought I heard a noise from one of the outbuildings. But I had lost the moment. I returned to the bedroom.

Smith came back in mid-afternoon. He had the decency to call on me at once, telling me that he had inspected some of his lands on the way to Belmont from Stony Point. He had not been born a farmer, but he chattered about crops and the need for rain after this scorching summer. His brother William, our Chief Justice in New York, had written to say that there was a severe water shortage in town. Had I any experience of the bottled water from Pennsylvania, and was it good for the digestion?

"No," I said. My stomach sounded.

Smith gave an embarrassed smile. He said, "I have neglected my duty as host." He bustled off and returned in a few minutes with a plate of cold meat, bread and salad, and tea to drink—one of the original sources of our Colonial disagreements. I asked him how he came to be here and his brother in New York, a way of saying why are you among the rebels and your brother with us; but he clearly desired to avoid this sort of conversation. "I was simply on this spot, and wished to go on with my life here, untroubled by events," he said. "Though that is difficult, as you see." He reverted to the visit of Mrs. Arnold on her way to Robinson's. "Such a pretty young thing, and so devoted to the General." The first half of that remark was obviously meant; the second might have borne the hint that it was amazing a girl so young should have engaged herself with so senior a man—or a hint that the devotion was less than it seemed. "Highly flirtatious, too," he added. I gave him a cool stare. His words provoked a picture of my host attempting to exact a return for his hospitality to the General's bride, perhaps by giving her a peck and a pinch. Or was this merely to be receptive to a somewhat prurient undertone in his voice? As if to make up my mind, Smith went on, "I can't think why you left Philadelphia, Mr. Anderson."

If this was intended to release from me a flood of reminiscence about my life in the city of brotherly and sisterly love, it failed. Once again I had a sudden wish that I could feel a genuine liking for the person with whom circumstances forced me to associate. Providence perhaps intended that, in this affair, I wait for that until I encountered you, Tallmadge. And perhaps I am now being unfair to Mr. Smith. I shouldn't antedate my distaste. He struck me then as someone who was really a city man, affecting to be a country gentleman; whose real desire was to get on with his petty pleasures as untouched as could be by political or military considerations. And yet easily flattered or bullied by someone like Arnold, who worked on his sense of self-importance and made him feel like the local squire. Mrs. Arnold one day, His Excellency General Washington the next, and the mysterious Mr. Anderson on vital commercial business not long after. Smith was needed; he and Belmont were on the edge of great events.

While I ate, Smith had been pacing past the window. Now he paused and looked out. His expression changed. A new care had arrived. I stood up and walked over to see what it was. The spars of the *Vulture* were once again in view. She now lay about a mile south of Teller's Point. I thought that there shouldn't be much difficulty about getting me back if she remained at anchor there. Perhaps twenty minutes longer to row than the voyage had taken Smith and his oarsmen the previous night. An ensign fluttered from the peak of the mainmast. In the distance, over the treetops, it was like one of those details that appear in the background of old paintings, curiously detached from whatever the central subject of the picture is.

I looked at Smith and read his mind. He had the grace to shift uneasily. Why did the man prefer the onerous privilege of accompanying me on a long ride to assisting me back to the *Vulture* by boat? Was he frightened by water? He excused himself; he would go and talk to the boatmen.

They must have been hard to find, for he was a long time gone. Yet despite what I knew to be their and Smith's reluctance, the *Vulture*'s presence kept the possibility of return by that way alive in my mind. Indeed, the *Vulture* positively hovered in my brain. I saw myself in the barge again, heard the oars moving, saw the starlight in the water, watched the shape of the ship's hull dissociate itself from the blur of night, and then the hail of a lookout, the rope ladder suspended and its wooden rungs in my hands, and at last Robinson's greeting: "We were getting a little impatient, André. But we never doubted that you would make it." I knew as I let my mind roam this way that it was unhealthy—an unlucky mode of thinking. When did you ever conceive of a happening in advance that turned out exactly as you conceived it? Or does the fact of it happening annul all such prior doubts and cogitations? My superstitious fear was that the preconception actually prevented the wished-for event from happening. I tried to think of something other. Leading the left wing of our forces up to West Point. Sir Henry's last letter to Lord George Germain, threatening resignation. A young woman who served in Tobias Stoutenburg's tavern in New York and who, on the last occasion I was there, accompanied me up to a vacant chamber and allowed me, oh so amicably, to have congress with her. Hendrickje her name. I had arranged to see her that Saturday—another reason for getting back to the *Vulture*. So the ship intruded into every fancy. The barge rowed out from the shore. The oars swung back and forth, and the pools of water that they made were swept astern, one by one by one.

I shall make a drawing of it, Tallmadge. John André being rowed down Hudson's river to the waiting ship. A memento. More I dare not. But forgive these whims.

When Smith returned, it was immediately evident that there were complications. He said that the Cahoon brothers resolutely refused to row again. Nothing would persuade them. Promises of money or flour were ineffectual; they would not be moved. He himself felt a bout of rheumatics coming on and did not relish the prospect of being on the water again in the night air. It would be just as well if we went by land, and what with the guard boats that would be watching the *Vulture* now, after the bombardment, we would have a much better chance of not being stopped for questioning, for even with passes from the General it was an irksome thing. "I'm convinced, Mr. Anderson, that if we cross at King's Ferry this evening, and ride on at an easy pace, you will be at the White Plains soon after daybreak tomorrow."

The objection that came to mind was insuperable, but perhaps delivered with hesitation, because I wondered for an instant whether it were rightly to be made by a man of commerce pretending to be an officer. "In that case, I would have to put off my uniform." Of course, the objection would still be made. The rub was that Smith, if he thought I was wearing the regimentals for show, as a display of self-

importance, would not treat it as a serious objection.
Why should a civilian mind donning civilian clothes
again?

In any event, he seemed to be prepared for it; had
no doubt thought of it while readying his remarks. He
said, "I'll lend you a coat. It may be a little large, but
will do for a night." There would naturally be no need
to change breeches, boots, or waistcoat, which had no
special marks identifying them as of military fashion.
Smith at this point had a turn of nervous jollity, pretending to measure my shoulders and arms like a
tailor. It occurred to me that he might very well be
scared; that the import of the transaction which
Arnold had been conducting with me had sunk in; and
that although he was attempting to continue to regard
it as commercial and possibly dubious (indeed everyone needed a second occupation in times like these;
even the Continental commander was said to fiddle his
account books; Congress's dollars were hardly worth
the paper they were printed on), he knew in the
depths of his plump being that what Arnold was up to
was something more serious. Perhaps on the ride to
the ferry he had been allowed a glimpse of the
General's ferocious self-interest. It was the kind of
passion from which Smith would instinctively recoil.
The timid neutral in him was preferring to stay on dry
land, presumably with more chance of hedging his
bets. I was not a favourite on whom he was prepared
to stake his all.

And yet the *Vulture* lay out there in the river, not
half an hour away! I wondered whether I should tell
Smith who I was. Would that frighten him more? It
struck me that perhaps it had entered his mind that
Arnold had brought me up here to discuss ways in

which I would act for him as an *American* agent?
Would he be friendlier if that were the case? The
other possibility was determined action on my part. I
could tie him up and make off into the woods, reach
the Hudson shore in the dark, and look for a boat in
Haverstraw. This did not seem like fitting behaviour,
however, when he was treating me as a guest in his
house. I tried to think of other impediments to his
proposal that could be mentioned.

"How will you provide me with a horse?" Had he
considered how he would retrieve his animal if I rode
off to New York on it? A horse was nothing to be
given away lightly in these days.

"General Arnold left one of his with me—Jupiter,
which he was riding last night. Elderly, but he'll get
you there."

It passed into my mind that Smith in thrifty fashion
was killing two birds with the one stone. He still had to
fetch his family from upriver. By going across at
King's Ferry and conducting me towards the Rebel
outposts north of the White Plains, he would be in a
position to swing back to Fishkill on his return journey
and collect his wife and children. But perhaps this was
unfair. Whatever the truth, it was the moment to put
on record my feelings for once and for all. I said, "I
would prefer the water route. I do not like the idea of
removing my uniform." I could not say, I have orders
not to remove my uniform.

But Smith obviously felt the matter had been
decided. Whatever his own nervousness, he did not
feel *my* danger. "My dear fellow," he said, with excessive cordiality, "do not distress yourself. You will
not be flaunting any irregularity. And we have the
General's pass."

That was true; the pass should serve. And Smith's tone reminded me that he was a local landowner, known in these parts. Attention would be paid chiefly to him as we made our way towards the lines. He brought me a jacket, a faded peach colour, with worn buttonholes and threadbare gilt trim at the lapels and cuffs. And when I turned to hang my regimental jacket on a peg behind the door, he took it down, saying with a smile, "I think it better that this does not remain on display." Even as he left the room with it, he was turning it inside out, as if hiding the telltale rich scarlet from his own corridors and stairs. I heard him go out into the yard. Without my uniform coat I felt wrong—and perhaps wronged. I knew Sir Henry would be shuddering if he knew.

You will perceive that I have been napping, Tallmadge. Falling asleep in the late afternoon, which is a sign of premature senility, or else of approaching winter and an animal need to curl up and keep warm. A more likely cause is that the fatigues of the past week are still catching up with me. I have just awakened to what I thought was the sound of bugles playing a retreat. I assume the camp at Tappan is not about to fold its tents and wigwams. Or has Sir Henry sent Simcoe and his rangers to rescue me? Go up to Tappan and retrieve John André! I admit dallying with this notion. Simcoe is about the only one of our officers who would rise to such a mission, but I don't think my good commander in chief would countenance the risk, even for his adjutant general. Moreover, it isn't his style these days. It might occur to him, but first he'd have to think about it for a week. He would want to confer with old Arbuthnot about the naval

side of the proceedings, and the Admiral would be
bound to make difficulties. "Not sure if the *Barbarian,*
a seventy-four, y'know, will serve. It might be better
to land a battery of guns at Sneden's to cover your
approach . . ." In the intricacies of organization they
would lose sight of the object of the manoeuvre. It
had not always been this way with Sir Henry. In the
assault on Verplanck's and Stony Point he showed
great initiative. But even then, as Governor Tryon has
been heard to say, there was no follow-through, no
general scheme, no system. This is obviously one
instance where I am with the wrong forces. You
Americans have brought off this sort of action very
cleverly—I am thinking of your abduction, three years
ago, of our General Prescott on Rhode Island, and of
his aide-de-camp Lieutenant Barrington, with only his
breeches on. If a general commanding four thousand
men, encamped on an island protected by a squadron
of ships of war, could be carried off from his quarters
at night, by a small enemy party, without a shot being
fired, why not me! Of course there were other influential factors—the intelligence received from the
inhabitants of the island, and their sympathy to the kid-
nappers' cause—which might not be the case in the
present instance. Still, with Simcoe in charge, or, even
better, General Arnold—there's the man for the task!
You would think he felt a debt of honour had to be
paid.

We set out from Belmont at half past six. I looked
at my watch; it was one of those moments when one
feels almost a naval need to keep a reckoning of when
one makes a landfall or takes a departure. Course
north-nor'west for Stony Point. There was a fresh
wind, a high scud of cloud, and the sky a blue-pink

to the west, where the sun was setting. Smith and I were accompanied by David, the groom. For a while the track was on marshy ground along the river. We turned inland for a short way, forded a brook which was nearly dry, then climbed a craggy ridge which we followed to within view of the Point. Smith had served up some fish stew before we left, and cider to drink. Smith's coat, under my cape, hung loose on me. I felt like a child wearing for play some parental garment. I wore also one of his plain round beaver hats (my cocked hat was still on the *Vulture*). Flexing my calf muscles, I could feel and almost hear crinkle Arnold's papers, which lined my boot. Perhaps sweat would make the ink run; perhaps I'd fall in the river, and that would put paid to them.

We journeyed for the most part in silence. Smith rode alongside me where the width of the road permitted it, and although we both made polite attempts now and then at conversation, neither of us had our heart in it. Silence was—tacitly!—agreed upon. The evening air had a touch of autumn in it. From elder and elm fell thin showers of yellow leaves; the maples were beginning to go red. Clouds of midges circled, lit by the long sunbeams, so dense you felt that you needed to duck under them, but so rarefied that you couldn't sense them when you brushed directly through the clouds. Over Purgatory Creek there was the small wooden bridge to cross, and then the dike, built up to carry the track across the marsh to the Point, a wooded promontory which is almost an island.

I had been here before, in May last year. Sir Henry had made one of his forays upriver, and I was sent across from Stony Point to receive the surrender of the Continental detachment at Verplanck's. We had possession for only six weeks before your General Wayne recaptured it. A bayonet charge by night! The sort of stroke that reminds us that this decidedly is a war. But even in war you lay your body down to sleep with peaceful thoughts, and take for granted that you will rise as usual to stretch your limbs come morning—not squirm in a final agony with a length of polished steel in your guts. As we rode past the outlying ditch and then the abatis and earthen bank that form the fortifications of the Point, I looked for the spot where I had camped last May. Isn't it so that there are many places to which you travel and then leave without consciously expecting to see them again? There are other times when you go to a spot and actually think, for some reason, "I wonder if I shall ever return here." As I came to Stony Point for the second time, I asked myself that question.

The picquet halted us at the top of the slope that leads down to the ferry. Smith identified himself. No attention was paid to me. At the landing, Smith gave a cheerful greeting to the men guarding the wooden blockhouse. One officer, who addressed Smith as "Jo," said that he might as well come and lodge with them, since he seemed to be spending much of his time coming to or crossing King's Ferry these days. Smith was invited to step in for a glass of grog and accepted.

"And what about your friend?" He gave a nod to me.

I shook my head and murmured my thanks. I would stay in the air, a slight fever . . .

I kept my distance until they went in; then I dismounted, gave the reins of the horse to David, and sauntered over to sit on a rock by the water's edge. I watched the ferry, in the last of the light, being rowed out from the far shore. The crossing here at the top of Haverstraw bay is—what would you say?—a bare half mile? The river narrows above here as it begins its more twisting course through the Highlands. Through here, God willing, Monday would see our ships come. I could make out only one six-pounder on this side of the crossing. I hoped to observe—if it were not too dark—where on Verplanck's Colonel Livingston had disposed his armaments. The keen fellow who had dislodged the *Vulture* with his gunnery. I knew Henry Livingston and he knew me, since he had guarded me for several days in the Canadian woods. If he saw me, would he recall my features after five years? Darkness on the other side of the ferry might be a friend.

Footsteps behind me. One of the rebel officers, glass in hand. He said, "You're not feeling well?"

I nodded, continuing to look out at the river.

"Jo Smith said you wanted to stay out of doors. The air is often heavy on the river at this time of day, certainly for one who is accustomed to sea breezes."

What had Smith been saying? "It's a touch of ague," I muttered, trying not to sound impolite, but also not encourage questioning.

"Riding does it to me. Something in the gait of some horses gives me the worst pain in the head and back."

What if this sympathetic man noticed that this was the steed General Arnold had ridden up here only this morning? What would his next question be? I tried to recall what I had decided in regard to the background of Mr. John Anderson. Philadelphia as my home had the advantage of greater distance from here. In my head I went over various commercial undertakings that I was currently employed upon, while at the same time affecting to listen to the American as he rattled on about a horse he had bought from one of the many teamsters who had passed King's Ferry recently. The supplies that were being brought downriver for the army at Tappan were landed at this point and loaded on wagons. The presence of the *Vulture* made it dangerous for them to do otherwise. But he thought that since this morning's success things might be different. Had I heard about it?

"No," I said.

The *Vulture* had been hit a number of times, he believed. Her rigging had been damaged, and one shot holed her between wind and water, and could have sunk her if it had struck her a foot or so lower, on the waterline. At any rate, the Colonel was really bucked and had recommended for promotion young Sam Tripp, who had been in charge of the battery. Sam had got himself a bit singed when the powder barrel blew up.

Fortunately, at this point the ferry drew in and Smith came forth, bidding his hosts a jovial farewell, waving to David to bring up the horses, and not giving the ferrymen a chance to get out of their scow. "Come on, lads, pull hard," he shouted cheerfully as they pushed off, "I'm on urgent business for the General." There were but two other passengers, a pair of ill-nourished-looking soldiers, returning to Verplanck's, who also encouraged the elderly oarsmen with good-humoured oaths. It was the last crossing of the evening. Let's see how fast you ancient sluggards can row.

None of this, of course, had much effect on those who pulled the sweeps. The ferry moved crabwise at a sluggish pace across the darkening river; as we approached the far side, under overhanging trees, it seemed dark enough to be the Styx. It was strange to be on the river—this same water in a little while would be flowing past the *Vulture*'s anchor rode and dividing around her timbered sides. If I could only have flowed with it! Hudson's without doubt was the thread upon which this whole tapestry depended. It was a pity that Sir Henry, who fitfully realized this fact, hadn't stuck with it as his controlling conception. We should have possessed the river and held the Highlands to the exclusion of all else. Forgotten about Charleston, Philadelphia, and Rhode Island. General Burgoyne should have been met and assisted from the south, with an army advancing upriver, and Lord Cornwallis should not have been sent off to exercise his separate ambitions in the Carolinas. He should have been made Lord of the Hudson, in order to control the route to Canada and command the passages, like this one, of men and goods between New England and the other colonies.

The scow grated on the landing. As we mounted, Smith said, "I'll just call on Colonel Livingston and pay my respects."

This seemed to me to be overdoing the courtesies, but there was no way I could prevent him. I rode twenty yards or so beyond the post and reined up. I gave Jupiter a pat on the neck; encouraging him, I encouraged myself. A few men moved past with a lantern, carrying pails of water, while others around a fire stood talking or smoking their pipes. No one paid any attention to me. From what little I could see as we rode through, the rebels had confidently levelled the fortifications we'd built there last year. I waited impatiently for Smith. Waiting, waiting! I assumed that he was doing what he felt he had to do and, being so well

known in these parts, would have drawn more attention if he had passed by without calling on Livingston.
And yet my skin bristled with apprehension. Surely
Livingston, being so close by, would sense the
presence of someone whom he had guarded for several
days in the north woods; we had talked of Congress
and Parliament, of my Lichfield and yours in Connecticut. I fully expected him to come out now and
look around. Indeed, the doorway of the house filled
with a man's shadow—one man appeared, then
another. But the second remained in the doorway, and
the first, Smith, walked to where David held his horse.
Smith trotted up alongside me as I moved on.

"I told him that I would not stay for supper," he
said. "I told him you was waiting, Mr. Anderson, and
that we were in a hurry to get off. He asked where we
were going, and I said up to Robinson's to see the
General."

This struck me as being in the way of a hostage
given: it might be information that Livingston soon
learned to be false, perhaps through a messenger arriving from Robinson's in the next few hours, perhaps
through having to go up there himself and finding that
we had not called there. However, it was no doubt
easy to say the first thing that came into one's head
when faced with a sudden question of that kind, only
later realizing that the answer had been foolish. I
believed that the right answer would have been one
closer to the truth, one that suggested we were travelling on business for the General, and that also suggested we couldn't, for confidential reasons, tell more;
that we were on an errand to gain information. I
waited for a few minutes so that the remark sounded

less immediately critical and then put to Smith the proposal that, if we were stopped, it might be better if he said something along those lines. He agreed.

On the road through the woods east of the river our horses made their own pace. Although there was no moon, the night was not pitch-black. From Verplanck's we headed northeast, for the moment towards Robinson's, on the beginning of a wide circle that would take us eventually east, then southeast, then south. We passed through Peekskill: a meetinghouse, a cluster of cottages. At the first fork thereafter we took the right-hand branch towards Crompond. Smith said that the route he favoured was one going to Pine's Bridge, across the Croton River. I was assuming that we would ride all night. The horses were fresh. There was no good reason why I should not by dawn have covered the twenty-four miles that lay between here and the safety of our lines at the White Plains.

It was a close night and the riding was warm. Not long after Peekskill, the rich, sweet smell of skunk enveloped the track—one of the natural wonders of the New World! Lord Rawdon, my predecessor as adjutant general, had been attacking the flanks of the Continental force near Germantown when he was sprayed by one of these small beasts. With such allies, the Americans hardly needed the French. We proposed to Rawdon various native remedies of which we had heard, such as sitting in baths of crushed tomatoes or apple cider, but he refused to indulge in anything other than hot water and scrubbing brush, and then cologne. It was at Germantown that some of the Rebels, when taken prisoner, were found to be drunk. I acknowledge that at least one of our generals, taken at any time of day, might be found in the same condition. I heard David laugh at something Smith said, perhaps about skunks. They were riding a little behind, as though Smith found his groom a better companion than the preoccupied John Anderson. But Anderson was feeling less out of sorts. The fact that we had passed two American posts without trouble was a help to my mood.

I reflected on Arnold. He and Peggy would be sitting down to supper now, and talking—would Arnold mention me? Probably not directly, but his mind with me at the back of it might turn to thoughts of Philadelphia, where he had kept a coach and four, and entertained the French ambassador at a public dinner. He would ask Peggy to tell him of what it had been like under the British occupation, and quiz her about her admirers among the King's officers. And this might lead to a remark about me. He would watch her expression as she responded. She would wonder why this subject came up at just this juncture and perhaps imagine that Arnold was jealous of her conquests before he came on the scene and conquered. She might stir him up a little with accounts of attentions paid to her. I doubted, however, that he would intimate to her his correspondences, his calculations, his meetings that day. My dear little Peggy was not to be bothered with serious matters like these.

"We're approaching Crompond," said Smith, riding nearer to me. Clear sky above and muted starlight. Away to the right in the woods an owl hooted. Smith asked, "Do you hear something? No, not the owl. Something on the road ahead?"

"Horses, sir," said David.

Yes, horses. Four of them drew up on the road ahead of us, barring the way. A tall figure in a dark

[73]

cape astride the nearest horse asked us to identify ourselves.

"Joshua Hett Smith and party," said Smith. "And you, sir?"

"Captain Boyd, New York Militia. You have some proof, sir?"

"I have passes here, Captain," said Smith. He handed over a paper, which the Captain took and held close to his eyes, twisting it as if to catch whatever light fell upon it, then saying, "This won't do. Come, there is a house at a short distance where we can examine this."

He and one of his men rode ahead of us; the other two, without being so ordered, came behind us. But it was not far to a house where a light was brought to the door. The Captain, his face underlit by the flame, read aloud: " 'Mr. Smith, Mr. Anderson, and servant.' " He looked at us in turn; he said to Smith, "And you are Smith?"

Smith had already identified himself, but he said with a nervous laugh, "Yes, indeed I am. From Belmont, on the other side of Hudson's."

"I see," said the Captain. His horse shifted its feet, an action which had the effect of moving it sideways and bringing Captain Boyd closer to me. His knee brushed mine. He talked across me to Smith: "Do you mind telling me your errand, Mr. Smith? Why are you travelling this way tonight?"

"Certainly, Captain." Smith then lowered his voice, perhaps to suggest that what he had to say was for Captain Boyd's ears alone. "General Arnold has employed me to accompany Mr. Anderson here towards the White Plains. We are meeting a gentleman near the British lines. We hope to receive useful information."

September 28

Boyd looked at me. The candlelight flickered. His eyes were deep-set in a gaunt face. We were much closer to each other than we would have been in daylight. I felt that he was close enough to hear me breathe and hear my heart pound. He said, "Mr. Anderson—then you are on the General's business?"

"That is right." I judged brevity to be the best mode of reply. I couldn't help but think of the papers in my boot, a few inches from the Captain's.

"You are not intending to ride all night, are you?"

Smith put in, "It was in our minds to do so—but we hadn't fully determined yet. I suppose we could stop at Major Strang's, if we decided to halt." This annoyed me. Of course we intended to ride all night! Why not say so?

Captain Boyd did not show that he was in any way impressed by the familiar way in which Smith had brought out Major Strang's name. He said coolly, "The Major is away from home. However, it would be advisable to go no further before daylight. It may well be dangerous below the Croton. We have reports that there are Cowboys out a-plenty."

I thought, Who cares about Cowboys? The pro-Tory freelance raiders would give me no anxiety if they took me as a captive into the British lines. If, on the other hand, the militia Captain had warned us about Skinners, the rebel volunteers who served the Continental cause by capturing cattle and terrorizing the Westchester countryside, that would indeed have been something to worry about, and a sound reason for halting for part of the night. But of course I couldn't say this to Captain Boyd. In a calmer state I might have admitted, moreover, that Cowboys and Skinners were less distinguishable; some of them moved back and forth, serving both armies as it suited their own interests. None were reliable.

"In the morning," Boyd continued, "you'll be better off on the North Castle road. It is the way by Tarrytown that they have infested."

I wondered whether the Captain was being sincerely helpful, or whether he felt a suspicion that made him want to delay us. He added, "You will ride on more assuredly after some rest."

I waited in vain for Smith to thank him for his advice and warning and to say that he would cautiously ride on now. We were accompanied by the Captain and his patrol for half a mile to a farmhouse, where the Captain himself went to the door to make evident to the farmer, an elderly Scotsman, that we were travellers of good character in need of shelter. The patrol did not move off until we had dismounted, the horses and David had been directed to a barn, and Smith and I had gone into the house.

From what you tell me, Tallmadge, tomorrow will be an important day. "The Proceedings of the Board of Officers" has an air of pomp about it. I wonder if I shall sleep. The mind on these occasions insists on preparing itself for all eventualities, going into all the nooks and crannies of possibility, though one knows from experience that it never quite foresees the circumstances that will pertain. One tends to dwell on the extreme events that may happen, imagining triumphs or disasters but not the more humdrum or ridiculous course that events ultimately take. The speeches that one makes in such insomniac speculation are rarely delivered. The amiable women whom one clasps to oneself in fancy are ill disposed when next encountered in reality.

At the Crompond farmer's—who would have guessed that the Scots farmer would be named Scott? —Smith and I were given a plate of porridge apiece. Our host had no meat; he had lost some cattle to Cowboys the week before. We were shown the whereabouts of the privy and then the loft, with its one rope bed. The stump of flickering candle was good for about two minutes, but before it had gone out Smith had collapsed with a weary groan on one side of the bed, pulling part of the quilt over him and saying, "Come on, Mr. Anderson, we will be up before dawn. At least take your boots off."

I waited for the dark before doing so. I felt the papers still inside them, and I placed the boots where they would be close to hand when I swung my legs out of bed onto the floor, in the event that I had to don them quickly during the night. Then I lay down and tried to soothe my agitated spirits. It was idiocy to be there in bed when I should have been riding on. I imagined myself heading towards the safety of our lines. And yet the figures of Captain Boyd and his men patrolled out there; perhaps they had gone down the road only a short distance and there waited, to make sure that we remained at Scott's. Part of my agitation arose from doubts as to whether I had been right not to assert myself: should I have had the confidence to overrule Smith and Boyd and tell them our mission was important, we had to go on?

From the sound of his breathing, Smith was asleep at once. An enviable facility. It also made the propinquity of his body less unsettling. Of course I have shared a bed on numerous occasions—it is a common feature of travel, especially during war. More than once I've woken to find another man's arm flung across my chest; perhaps in his dreams he was caressing his mistress. But however often it is said to happen in the navy, buggery has been suggested to me only once— a drunken fellow officer, whom I kicked out onto the floor, and who had, so it appeared, no memory of it next morning.

I could feel the ropes through the thin straw-filled pallet, forming a gridiron. If I turned on my side, the area exposed was smaller. After a while, I thought, I might try the floor. For a long time my mind went on fretting over all manner of eventualities. And at last I found myself apologizing to the Creator for the self-concerned and, coming from me, unlikely offering of a prayer: Lord, let me fall asleep.

TAPPAN

Friday, September 29

1780

Why, whom do we have here? No Tallmadge today, but Lieutenant King. I assume Major Tallmadge has duties connected with the Board of Officers. But having to look after me here must strike you as preferable to having to ride with me all night in pelting rain, as we did when last in company. This morning since first light I have been drawing and writing, impelled by a sense of *vita brevis* and a hope of organizing my thoughts. No doubt you will give me warning of when to prepare myself for the proceedings, that is, to prepare my dress. My account is now as prepared as it can be. One trouble that I have been having is determining the truth of my story—I have been going back over things and contemplating what would have happened if I had done such-and-such differently. Sometimes the alternative action assumes a firm place in my mind, replaces that which in fact occurred; though sadly, all actions, real and hypothetical, lead here. And I still find difficulty in totally believing that this is indeed how things are. I have pinched myself again. *This is not a bad dream.* This is not even a play in which I am merely a bad actor, or in which I would

[*81*]

have the ability to alter some of the lines. Suddenly my destiny seems remorseless.

Last Saturday I was up at five. I shook Smith awake and went to the barn to tell David to make ready the horses. Farmer Scott offered us some breakfast, but before Smith had a chance to agree I declined it. I said we must be off at once, and then, if we had made good progress, would perhaps get something to eat at a house along the road. I hoped we would not run into Captain Boyd and his men again this morning. Smith gave the farmer a few Continental dollars for our lodging and then we were away, trotting towards Pine's Bridge in the cool near-darkness that precedes the dawn.

I felt remarkably affable as with the daylight we approached the Croton river. South of it I would be for certain in no-man's-land, unlikely to run into any American patrols. I had a sensation of lightness, of floating along, which may have been an effect of a night in which I had dozed occasionally but had been awake much of the time. The day began grey and hazy. The countryside was scrappy, mostly wooded, but with here and there a field ill tended, surrounded by rough stone walls, or an orchard in need of care. A land in need of able menfolk, now elsewhere. I saw a quince tree near the road and it reminded me of the one that grew in the garden at home, and the tart taste of quince in apple pie. I was friendly with Smith. He was less inclined to be talkative this morning and perhaps surprised that I was instead. I chatted about anything that came to mind. For some reason I remembered a stage ride back from Lichfield when we lost a wheel and an Irish carter stopped and kindly offered us assistance. To this Samaritan our coachman was confoundedly and rudely ungrateful, and I had felt a compulsion to make up for it—at which point the carter had spurned my thanks, oblivious to everything except his own hurt feelings. How tied up we are in our own pride! Smith asked about the prevalence on our roads of highwaymen, and seemed disappointed that I had no personal experience of these gentlemen, other than once having seen one of them hanged at Tyburn.

Bien-être allowed me to feel that satisfying our hunger would now be no great sacrifice of time. "Shall we breakfast here?" I said to Smith as we approached a cottage from whose chimney smoke was rising. At least Smith showed no surprise that my compulsion to get on had faded before the imperative of an empty stomach. Our hostess was an elderly Dutch *vrouw*; she possessed a cow and a vegetable patch, and offered to her visitors the porridge that appears to be the staple of these parts. I ate two hearty helpings and drank a little fresh milk, and put aside as well as I could any thoughts of eggs and ham. Tonight, coffee at the King's Arms! Once again Smith paid. Before we remounted, he handed over to me the passes Arnold had made out and most of the paper money he had with him. Eighty Continental dollars. "It may buy you dinner," he said. "From here, Pine's Bridge is scarcely a mile. If you'll permit me, I'll turn back there."

He may have been feeling the urgency of his promise to collect his family from Fishkill; he may have been simply taking advantage of my cheerful mood—it did not matter. South of Pine's Bridge, he— if one gave him the benefit of neutral sympathies— might feel increasingly ill at ease. I would be just as well alone on the remainder of the journey. And therefore, when we reached the crest of a hill overlooking the Croton river, as it ran westwards to join Hudson's under Teller's Point, I reined in. No need to make Smith go any further. I felt for the moment nearly grateful to him, despite his failure to return me to the *Vulture*. I said, "Will you call in at Robinson's?"

"I will inform the General you are well on your way."

"And I will return your coat and the money to your brother's in New York."

"I doubt if he will find the coat useful. But give him my best wishes. It is some time since we met." He did not say: I trust he and I will be meeting soon. He was preserving his ambivalence to the last. He looked up and down the road, clearly itching to set forth on his return journey along it. I shook his hand. Catching David's eye, and getting a smile, I gave the groom a word of thanks and a wave of farewell. They turned and rode north.

I looked at my watch; it was seven o'clock. Then I set Jupiter in motion downhill towards the bridge. I was on my own! I chanted aloud:

> *O'er hills and dales and bogs,*
> *Through wind and weather*
> *And many a hair-breadth 'scape,*
> *We've scrambled hither.*

It was from the prologue to a play—a thoroughly preposterous play—I had helped put on in Philadelphia. The hooves of the horse clattered over the planking of the bridge. From my position in the saddle, the water seemed a long way below. If I had been in New York this morning I would have found time to call in at Rivington's bookshop and pick up a copy of his gazette, out today. It contained the last section of my ballad *The Cow-Chase*, which celebrated, albeit comically, the martial prowess of your General Wayne. With the freedom of the road I proclaimed:

> *And pack-horses with fowls came by,*
> *Befeather'd on each side,*
> *Like Pegasus, the horse that I*
> *And other poets ride.*

Perhaps I was a bit bold to call myself a poet, even tongue-in-cheek. I could have written: "And other scribblers ride." But then the classical allusion would have seemed less apt.

"Come on, Jupiter-Pegasus," I said, patting my steed alongside his mane, where there were grey hairs among the chestnut, urging him into a faster walk. Beyond the bridge the road followed the Croton for half a mile before veering south, beside a brook. It wound through small hills, past ponds, marshy ground, and the occasional cleared field. It was bumpy, irregular country, interspersed with woods. Hardscrabble Road, Smith had called it when advising me about the route to follow, and hardscrabble it looked. The few farmhouses along the way appeared to have been abandoned, with their shutters nailed shut and weeds growing high in front of the doors. Before the Rebellion this had been prosperous land, leased out by great estate owners like the Philipses, Beverley Robinson's relatives, and the Delanceys, the family of my good friend Oliver, for cultivation by small farmers. At what I calculated to be about fifteen miles to the White Plains, I came to a junction, with several cottages, a horse trough, and a well, from which a small boy was hoisting a bucket.

"How busy is the road to the White Plains this morning?" I asked the child, while Jupiter guzzled water from the trough.

The boy didn't reply for a moment. Was he addled or merely cautious of strangers? Or was he simply trying to remember what he had seen so far today? He suddenly said, "Aye, some scouts went that way."

"Continental scouts?"

"Yup."

"When?"

"Within the hour."

So it was just as well I had asked. I said, "And how far is it to Tarrytown by the other road?"

" 'Bout four miles, sir."

It was in that direction that I set off, after Jupiter had munched a few mouthfuls of grass and wildflowers growing by the trough, heading along the road towards Hudson's river to join the post road down to Tarrytown. It was a longer way, and that which Captain Boyd had said was infested with Cowboys— but they were preferable to the Yankee marauders as far as I was concerned.

You say that I am required in an hour, in the stone church next door. Will there be a religious service as well? A pleasantry, friend King. I will not powder my hair. I wonder, however, if at this stage I should suggest that it would be a decided kindness if my red coat were retrieved from the Smith house. Or is that a poorly timed request, in that it might attract attention to the fact that I indeed put off my coat? Perhaps it would be better for me to postpone the suggestion until later today.

. . .

September 29

After the pause for watering, the road was undulating and well wooded on either side; most trees still green, though a few beginning to turn to those vivid colours that signal autumn on this continent. Jupiter rocked along easily, whether going uphill or down, and I let myself fall at ease into a loose-backed seat, swaying with the horse's motion. Now and then Jupiter gave a grumpy snort as he reached the summit of an ascent, but he didn't slow down. The only sounds came from his hooves crunching as they landed on pebbled patches of the dirt road, the flutter of a few leaves descending, and birds aroused into flight by my passing. I undid my cape and strapped it behind the saddle; the day was warm by half past eight. It seemed to me that there must be far worse ways of spending a late September morning than this, with the sun beginning to burn through in the sky, with each breath I took seeming to add to my good spirits. Together with this physical elation I had a sudden surge of affection for this country. I felt at home in it. Just below a hamlet called Sparta, where the road from Pine's Bridge joined the post road coming down from Albany, I drew up to glimpse the river to the west. Not a jot of evidence of warfare was to be seen. Here I could purchase acres, clear the ground, build a house, and paint and write. I could bring my mother and sisters over to make up my family. I could make trips to the city when the craving for amusements overtook me. Drickje.

I had been riding down the post road only ten minutes or so when another rider appeared, coming north. There was no chance of turning off or hiding. We would have to pass each other. Keep going, I said to myself, don't hesitate or look excited. The on-

coming horseman was on a big bay, and at twenty
yards I recognized him. He was a Rebel officer who had
been our prisoner in New York for several years but
who had been eventually released on parole. I had
interviewed him a year ago: Colonel Samuel Webb, of
a Connecticut regiment. And just as I knew him, so
surely he would know me. All I could hope was that
the unfamiliarity of the circumstance would work in
my favour. The British adjutant general would hardly
be expected to come riding south through no-man's-
land.

We closed rapidly, like knights in a fairy tale, our
steeds clip-clopping towards each other. At our
Mischianza in Philadelphia a mask or a paper helmet
and visor had been appropriate costume for our
Knights of the Blended Rose, Knights of the Burning
Mountain. Our motto: Only the brave deserve the
fair. I wondered for an instant if I could contort my
face, puffing the cheeks, stretching the mouth, narrow-
ing the eyes to visorlike slits, so that I would be
unrecognizable. I wondered if I should give him a
hail-fellow-well-met greeting, but at once dismissed as
foolish anything that might involve stopping for conversation. Then we were hard upon each other. Webb
was smiling in surprise, saying "Good morning!" And
I was giving him a nod and the cool sort of "Good
day" you might give a complete stranger. I didn't dare
look around as he went past. I knew he was looking
back at me. He had recognized me and must have been
thinking, What is *he* doing out here? But the sounds
of his horse faded behind me.

I spurred Jupiter into faster motion for a while. It
might be interesting to see how Colonel Webb con-
strued the terms of his parole if he shortly encountered

some Continental scouts, whom it would be possible to send after me. Yet from what I had observed so far this morning I thought the chances of him meeting scouts were small, and even if he did, that he would not mention running across me. The morning, as you can tell, was still working its magic on me. All was for the best. The world was suffused with sun, birdsong, a light breeze. Soldiers have to take their pleasures while they can, never knowing when a general, intending an expedition, is going to post them aboard the transports and leave them to rot in the harbour while he awaits news of enemy movements or word from Lord George Germain. And then the weather changes, or his mind changes, or Lord George fails to write, and he brings them ashore again. A soldier overeats when he can because he may be on short rations for weeks thereafter. He sleeps when the regiment is allowed to halt because it may be marching, or furnishing him as a guard, all night. He drinks his fill from the first clear brook, because his canteen may run dry, or be stolen by one of his mates, and there may be no brooks to drink from for miles to come.

We playacted in Philadelphia after having taken part in bayonet charges at Germantown, where death was real, dying painful on both sides; the acting was a necessary compensation. We were fighting a war which was not clear-cut. Poor Lord Howe was given commands by Whitehall to attack the Americans in such-and-such a way at one moment and counter-orders to present them with peace proposals on such-and-such a score the next. No wonder he gave the impression that he and the King's forces did not know whether they were coming or going. Sometimes I felt that reality was in fact there on stage, in the John

Major André

Street theatre, as we again performed *The Beaux'*
Stratagem. In that play I was Archer, a gentleman of
broken fortune, and affecting to be the servant to his
friend Aimwell, who is romantically attached to
Dorinda, Lady Bountiful's daughter: I was acting a
character who is acting another. Most men try to make
daily life acceptable by letting their imaginations roam
in fantasies of fame and fortune and amorous adven-
ture. In the theatre we make a similar attempt to set
aside humdrum routine, but our fantasies, jointly produced, are more real, bodied forth by the actions of
the actors. Take John Anderson—we could make a
play about him. Born in England, in Richmond, let us
say, the natural son of Colonel Sir Andrew Bennett,
baronet; his mother a French actress who for conven-
ience marries a kind gentleman of the city (or should
she be his housekeeper, like Mrs. Baddeley, Sir Henry
Clinton's good friend?). After an education mostly
abroad, young John, prompted by his earnest foster
father's wishes, sails to Philadelphia and is employed
in a merchant's house, where tea and fine cloths are
imported. He falls in love with a young belle, Elizabeth, whose family are a mainstay of local society, but
who is already betrothed to the thrusting shipowner
Samuel Needham. A rebellion breaks out. Anderson's
sympathies are with the Rebels, a fact which gives
displeasure to Elizabeth and her family, who are
staunch Loyalists. Anderson is called to the flag and
—through Needham's secret influence—is sent to a
regiment engaged in battle; in the corner of a field
(stage left, staggering on), he finds himself locked
in single combat with a senior officer parted from his
rank and file. It is none other than—though he does

[*90*]

not yet know it!—his father, Sir Andrew. Their sabres clash . . .

I was amusing myself in this manner as I rode towards a rough log bridge spanning a stream. On the far side, the road passed through a clump of trees forming a densely shaded covert or grove; sycamores and chestnuts growing tall, and thick bushes beneath. It is funny how the mind and senses work. In my head I was still pursuing my play while my eyes perused this landscape, and I felt—or at least half of me felt, half of me still being on stage—that I had seen this grove many times. I had played in it as a child—had wandered in it as a youth, following my own thoughts, and taken a girl into it for kisses. A place one came to for joy or for sorrow. I crossed the bridge, and the brook sparkled beneath. A lovely morning.

"Halt there!"

I brought up short. My hands tugged the reins to arrest Jupiter. A man stood beside the road wearing a Hessian Jaeger's jacket. Two others stood behind him. All with muskets. Uncouth fellows—as it were, stage right, the part of my mind that was still in the theatre insisted. In fact, villainous-looking creatures, but Cowboys, I was sure.

"It's all right, men, be easy," I said. "You have the appearance of belonging to the right party." I could hear my own words echo, as in a theatre that is empty when the play is being rehearsed.

It seemed that my remark wasn't heard. The man now holding Jupiter's bridle, a few paces beyond the bridge, continued to look at me. I wondered if he was drunk. Then he said, "And which is that?"

"Of course the lower party."

He looked at his companions and nodded. "Ah, that we are."

"And so am I." The words escaped me with relief. "You must let me pass."

He looked again at his companions. One of them winked and smiled. Another was staring at my boots in the way a hungry man might look at a prospective dinner. I reminded myself that volunteers were by no means trained soldiers. No sergeant major had put them through their paces. I said firmly, "I am on urgent business and must not be detained."

"Is that so?" The Jaeger-jacketed fellow grinned. "In that case, Mr. Urgent Business, we propose that you get down and tell us your lower-party errand."

The proposal was backed by the lifting of a musket. I dismounted. I did so as slowly as I could, rebuking myself and collecting my scattered wits. I had ridden into an ambush and compounded the peril by assuming that these men were Cowboys. Better to have thought that they were Macheath and company! Amends had to be made swiftly. I said, "Gentlemen, I'm happy to see that I was wrong. I was expressing what it seemed best to say, since I expected to find men of the lower persuasion along this route. In fact, I bear General Arnold's pass. I'll show it to you. I am in his service."

"Damn Arnold's pass!"

This came from one of the pair who were standing back. However, his associate came forward to take the pass, which I ought to have produced to begin with; he glanced at it with the indifferent, almost superior look of one who cannot read, and with a "Here, Paulding" handed it to Jaeger-jacket, their leader. He —Paulding—gave the control of Jupiter to the other and scanned the paper; he looked at me and said,

"How do we know how you came by this?" He approached closer. Small light-blue eyes, dark stubble on his chin. He said, "Take your clothes off, sir. We mean to search you."

"I have only a small amount of money upon me," I said. "It is yours if you require it. And I have this watch. Take that, too, if you must. But I ask you then to let me get on. The General's business is urgent, as I said."

The watch was snatched from me and rubbed to make its gold case shine. The man Paulding said in a mocking tone, "The General's business will have to keep. Williams, you start on him at the top. Van Wart, take off his boots. Let's see what he has got."

In these last few days I have been reliving those moments particularly. The foolishness—the humiliation—the failure of mind on my part that had brought this about. How quickly a daydream becomes a nightmare. My toes curl again, as they did then, resisting the tug on my boots. A sharp chop with a hand on the side of my left thigh made me relax my hold. My shoulders stiffened inside my coat, but it was lifted above my shoulders and pulled from my arms. I was sensible of all this, but it seemed to be happening to someone else, perhaps the lamented Anderson. I was in a stupor caused by my own idiocy. I was thick with shame at my slowness. I felt as if I were under water, unable properly to see or hear, with everything around me blurred and obscure. There was a pounding pressure within me. The boots were off, but had for the moment been set aside. They were looking through the pockets of my breeches and waistcoat, tugging at the lining of Smith's jacket, and searching the saddle.

My hose were pulled off. It was like being dismembered by a creature with many arms.

The one going through my jacket said, "He's not rich, Paulding. No specie here. Eighty miserable dollars."

"The watch is fine," said the other, still fingering it.

Paulding snapped, "Look in his boots! Haven't you done that yet? Get on with it!"

And that was it. The smaller henchman, van Wart, pulled forth the thin sheaf of papers. For a second I thought he was going to throw them over his shoulder in disgust, but Paulding snatched them, leafed through them, read them slowly, recited several phrases aloud, and then looked at me with malicious pleasure. "A real stroke of fortune," he said. "Here's something worth a good few British pounds, I reckon."

This brought me to the surface; a chance of air, of life. Money might do the trick. I heard myself saying that, as they could see, I did not have a deal of it with me, but that I could put them in the way of being well rewarded. If they cared to deliver me to King's Bridge, at the top of New York island, they would be able to name the proper sum.

Paulding appeared to be thinking of this for a moment. The papers had disappeared into a pocket of the Jaeger's jacket. Then he snorted, "Huh! If we took you to King's Bridge, we'd find ourselves in the Sugar House with a flogging. And you'd save your money."

Indeed, the Hessian jacket would probably get him hanged for a spy. But letting my mind drift to that sort of outcome, however desirable, would do me no good at this moment. I mustered all the eagerness and forthrightness the situation permitted and said, "In that case, I can only promise you fair dealing and this proposition: if I remain with two of you, the other can take to New York a letter I will write, which will ensure safe conduct through the lines, to and fro. You may name the price."

For a few minutes they muttered together. At last Paulding said, "A thousand guineas might do."

I hesitated. I wondered whether agreeing to this would make me and my errand seem too valuable to myself—so valuable, in fact, that they might feel obliged to hand me over, not at King's Bridge, but to the side which, after their own interests, they principally favoured. It could be too big a thing for makeshift highwaymen. But I had no choice. If I began to haggle, they might just as easily lose patience and determine to take me to the Rebel forces for a reward. I said, "I agree. Your price is undeservedly high, but if you swear to return me to King's Bridge in the end, I will see that it is yours."

Once again they held a mumbled consultation at a slight distance, while one of them kept the musket aimed at me. There was, I gathered, some disagreement between Williams and van Wart. I heard Paulding refer to having been captured by the British and then having escaped, only a few days before. He wasn't going to put *his* head back in the noose. I sat by the roadside, thinking that none of them looked sane. In the end Paulding swore at the other two and broke away. He confronted me. He kicked my thigh. A rude fusillade of words poured forth. They did not go along with my proposal. If they did, and tried to exchange me for a reward, the British would no doubt pursue them with a troop of dragoons. In any event, they were Yankee patriots, with higher motives. They had decided to carry me to the nearest American officer

commanding on the line. With a final sneer Paulding
said, "You may put on your boots. Then we'll ride."

I have had six days to think about it—to think of
little else! What would you have done, Mr. King, if
you had been in those boots? One course of action
that should have occurred to a professional soldier was
to enforce my own death, then and there. I had no
weapons, but an attack on the three Skinners, or an
attempt to escape, might have led them to shoot me
down, and that at least would have ended my participation in this sorry affair. But it was not a morning
notable for presence of mind on my part, or heroism;
the idea did not strike me. Moreover, one clings to
hope. Fate which had dealt me such a hand one
moment might decide to treat me with kinder fortune
the next. Again, I might have better luck with General
Arnold's pass when brought before a regular officer
accustomed to respect such articles. Arnold had said
that he had a week before warned several of his outlying posts to expect a Mr. Anderson passing through.
Then the papers he had given me might suddenly
acquire a sound reason for being in my possession.
What would *you* have said about them?

You must forgive me for going on with my remembered journey while I breakfast. How I miss the hot
cakes we used to have in the mornings in Geneva,
covered in butter; and our London muffins, with the
honey soaking in. Yet I suppose this coarse bread of
yours is good for the digestion. I have been told that
the Comte de Rochambeau's men insist on baking their
own from their own flour. If your allies are that way
with their food, how will they be on the field of battle?
But the journey—it was twelve miles or more across

country to the Continental outpost of North Castle, to which I was taken. My captors preferred to avoid roads where they might have encountered Loyalist patrols or other ruffians like themselves out for booty. I heard them bickering about the comparative worth of my watch, saddle, bridle, and horse, and about my value. Skinners they were indeed, and well named. Sometimes I sat in the saddle with my eyes closed. To think was painful, and to see was more so. With the sun over my right shoulder, my shadow fell to the north, and the sight of it rebuked me with the fact that I was going aslant the course I had intended to pursue. I was no longer on Jupiter but on the least favoured of their own nags. Paulding was astride Jupiter. If the venerable horse had had the wit, he would have bolted or thrown his rider; but he went on in civil fashion, heedless of whether he was ridden by American general, British major, or Skinner chieftain. Just before noon we joined the Bedford road below North Castle. The Continental post had been installed in a small, single-storey house in the centre of the village. Over the door a sign recalled the owner and previous occupant, Ebenezer S. Niles, attorney.

Paulding hitched Jupiter's reins to a post and went into the house without a word, leaving me in the custody of his colleagues. When he reappeared after a few minutes, he was looking sullen; perhaps he'd been told there was not to be an immediate division of the spoils. He shouted to van Wart, "Take the gentleman in. Lieutenant Colonel Jameson will see him." He seemed to spit rather than speak the words "gentleman" and "Lieutenant Colonel."

I was ushered into a small hall and then into a room with wainscotting and a wide fireplace. An officer I assumed to be Jameson stood up, and for a moment looked as if he were about to shake my hand. He was a large man, about my age, with a jutting chin, heavy eyebrows, and a gaze that seemed preoccupied. He spoke in a Virginian accent, with a touch of irritation, giving the impression that this development was one more thing come to burden him on an already busy day. "Your name, sir?"

"John Anderson."

"And this is your pass, which I have received from the volunteers?"

"Yes."

"It says: 'Permit Mr. John Anderson to pass the guards to the White Plains, or below if he chooses, he being on public business by my direction.' And then General Arnold's signature."

"Yes. I must say, it does not seem to have carried much weight so far."

Jameson ignored this remark. "And these other papers, sir, that were found on you, I gather in your boots?"

"I cannot speak of them, except to General Arnold."

Jameson looked down at the sheaf of papers on his table, lying alongside an unlit pipe full of dark tobacco. Behind him, an uncurtained window allowed me to see a horse shed and a yard in which men were lounging and playing cards. Jameson went on: "You see my difficulty, I hope. The name of Anderson was made known to me. I was informed that a Mr. Anderson would present himself at one of our posts. But the circumstances in which you were found—the direction you were taking—the papers in your boots . . ." He looked at me and, when no further explanation was forthcoming, said, "Well, sir?"

"There were problems that had not been foreseen."

"That does not answer my questions. I would like to know how these papers came into your possession."

"I can only tell General Arnold."

"Where were you going?"

"To the General. I had been going north, but heard of Cowboys on the road ahead. So I was returning to Tarrytown, meaning to turn east there and take a more circuitous route to the General. When I was stopped, I thought the men were Cowboys and attempted to persuade them that I was sympathetic to their cause, that they might let me continue."

Jameson toyed with his pipe. He walked with it to the fireplace and back again. He said, "In whose employ are you?"

"I am on business the General will acknowledge."

"Are you a military man?"

"Indeed not. I would hardly put myself in this situation, in this dress, if I were." My voice perhaps wavered, but I hoped that it sounded as though it did so from a sense of injury.

"And where do you reside, sir?"

"My home is in Philadelphia, but I am now travelling on business and agreed to seek information for the General."

"I see."

Plainly Lieutenant Colonel Jameson did not see. He sat down at the table and looked at the pass and then at the papers. It struck me as I saw them lying side by side—*both pass and papers were in Arnold's hand.* Jameson must surely recognize the same penmanship in both. But so far he had not. In fact, he put the pass to one side, the papers to the other, like business that needed separate decisions. He said abruptly, "Sit down, Mr. Anderson. You look fatigued. Have you been riding long?"

"A fair while, sir." I attempted to make this vague answer sound positive and friendly, in response to Jameson's more sympathetic manner.

"I will arrange for you to be given something to eat. Our provisions are not ample here."

I thanked him for his courtesy. And I was inspired to add, "The General promised me a feast when I reached him."

Jameson lit his pipe. He watched the smoke rise and seemed to be pleased by the sight. He said, "Well, when Lieutenant Allen returns later on, he will escort you to General Arnold."

"I'm much obliged, sir."

"Of course, you will be under guard, and I am compelled to let the General know of the curious manner in which you arrived here."

I nodded, to signify that I realized this would be necessary. I took hope from Jameson's tone of voice: a shade of war-weariness could be heard, I thought. He was therefore going through a procedure; this was not his sort of thing, and he wanted to be shut of it as soon as possible. It was evidently Arnold's affair— either this Anderson was working for the General, in which case the General should sort it out, or he was working against the General, and the General should know about it in good time. It might well be a British plot to embarrass the American commander at West Point. On the other hand, Arnold had mentioned Anderson's coming . . . Jameson handed me back the pass. The papers remained on the table. I didn't dare mention them. I wanted to keep my small flame of hope alight, and a renewal of distrust might snuff it out. Get me to Arnold as soon as possible!

It was mid-afternoon when I set out again, this time guarded by Continental regulars: a young lieutenant named Allen and four shabby-looking dragoons. I had spent several hours on a bench in Attorney Niles's back room, had eaten a few bites of extremely salty fish, brought to me by a trooper, and had then dozed from sheer exhaustion. Before I was sent off, there was another brief interview with Jameson. The post commander declared that it was a pity that his second-in-command, Major Tallmadge, was out on patrol; the Major usually concerned himself with these matters. "These matters" presumably meant persons turning up in rather curious circumstances with questionable documents—the papers were no longer in view on Jameson's table. I was glad of the Major's absence. I had heard of him. He apparently served the Americans in Westchester, collecting information from those who managed to move back and forth across the lines. Some of Major Tallmadge's correspondents in New York were no doubt people who had offered to sell information to me. Although Jameson had not as yet jumped to any conclusions about "these matters," Tallmadge with his experience in that region might be less hesitant.

As my escort arrived at the door, Jameson said with cautious courtesy, "I will look after your horse and possessions until we receive word about you. It may be, if you pass back this way, you can collect them then."

Leaving North Castle, I was treated to a last sight of the brigands who had brought me in. The three of them were sitting on the steps of the meetinghouse, rolling dice. They were obviously aware that I was going past, under escort, for I heard one of them say, as the dice rolled, "A thousand guineas!"—at which his companions laughed, though they kept their eyes down. No doubt they meant to remain in the vicinity of Jameson's post until word came back. And if Mr. Anderson turned out to be what they thought he was, they would claim his watch and horse as their rightful prize.

Lieutenant Allen rode alongside me; two men were in front, two behind. It is hard for men to ride together hour after hour without conversing, but Allen remained taciturn; the ambiguity of my situation perhaps rendered him so. I was then, and continue to be, impressed by the attention to military correctness shown by this impoverished army of rebellious farmers and merchants. The evening was grey and close; it threatened thunder. I'd been put on a temperamental mare, instead of the placid Jupiter, and the beast seemed to be affected by the weather. It was almost comic at the first fork we reached in the road to have to tug her around in the direction Allen was taking, and not let her go in the direction she wanted, setting her to a gallop and waiting for the pursuit and gunfire to begin. Escape (or an attempt at it) occurred to me. But I thought that my best chances lay in reaching Arnold as soon as possible. I wished, however, that I knew where the wretched papers were. Was Allen carrying them to hand to Arnold, or had Jameson kept them, in order to consult Tallmadge about them when he returned?

I gave my attention to my mount as thunder began

to rumble somewhere off. I generally rode with no great zest; rode because I had to, and because, lacking a chaise, a stage, or nowadays a canal boat, it was the best means of transport from one place to another. One learns to ride as one learns to crawl or walk. I was never in receipt of compliments as a natural rider, although my father's groom, Kemp, worked hard on me as a youth, and soon enough the reins disposed themselves properly in my hands, my back was straight, and I learned to keep my seat down, my weight low, my knees pressed in, my heels not sticking out, and to remember umpteen other do's and don't's of equestrian etiquette. Kemp was there to haul me out of the stable muck on the occasion I slithered over a horse's neck. Kemp—perhaps just as well—was not on hand when I went alone for the first time into city streets and was thrown, my steed having been frightened by a wildly careering carriage. Kemp had gone from us—my father dead, horses hired as needed from the local livery—when I was taken for my first hunt, outside Lichfield. It was terror mixed with pleasure of a kind, chasing over the hedges, in my case pleasure mostly at still being in the saddle at the end of the day. Hedges were being planted everywhere, enclosing the old fields, as if to increase the need for jumping every minute or so. These hunts are like miniature wars, in which you eventually may run to earth an outnumbered enemy a good deal smaller than most of the creatures chasing him. Good experience for cavalry officers, perhaps. Honora and Anna thought that hunting was both stupid and cruel. Sir Henry, my commander, is fond of arranging drag hunts, up to Kips Bay or the village of Greenwich, where the last time we passed through all the local mongrels joined in. I'm not much of a one for yoicking and tallyhoing, I'm afraid.

We came up the road to Pine's Bridge as it set in to rain. I had not expected to see Pine's Bridge again, at least not so soon. Or was it soon? In some ways that morning already seemed a lifetime away. The rain filled the air like a thick warm mist, and we were soon saturated. Allen said suddenly, "We might as well jump in the Croton and have a bathe." Possibly he surprised himself, addressing me in this familiar and spontaneous way. I replied that I thought a good deal more rain was needed to make the Croton deep enough for swimming. We passed the old Dutch woman's cottage, where Smith and I had breakfasted, and not long after the farmhouse where we had spent the night. I saw the old Scotsman coming in from one of his fields, but he paid no attention to the passing horsemen; he had doubtless seen enough of them for a lifetime. There was no sign, thank God, of Captain Boyd and his men. We passed a roadside gibbet, with the bones of a man hanging in chains, that I hadn't noticed in the dark the night before. Allen muttered, "One of Colonel Sheldon's men." A deserter, I assumed. Men seemed to desert in tidal currents, from us to them, from them to us. Our deserters are most often ordinary soldiers disgusted with the tribulations of army life, or perhaps seduced by the prospect of American land; while the Rebel deserters are often officers returning to their proper allegiance, so one could scarcely term it desertion, but frequently caused by indignation at their uncertain pay and deplorable conditions.

September 29

We were nearly at Peekskill when one of the men riding in the rear shouted, "Mr. Allen! *Whoa*, sir!"

We stopped and looked back. A rider was coming up at a canter behind us. Allen trotted a little way to meet him. There was a short conversation between them in the growing dark. I let my mind float into the branches of the trees that overhung the road, avoiding speculation about message and messenger. Nothing good could come from a change of plan. Then Allen rode back to us and said, "Mr. Anderson, we are to return to North Castle."

There was not a word on the ride back. If the atmosphere had been correct before, it was chilly now. I would have liked to see Allen show some annoyance at the new order, which countermanded our journey to Robinson's House; we had ridden to Peekskill and back for no reason. But he showed no emotion. I asked for no explanation. I was sure that none would be given.

North Castle again, and again: "Will you give me your name, profession, and purpose of your journey?"

"John Anderson, merchant. I am on confidential business, which General Arnold will explain to you."

"In the meantime, sir, might you explain how—if you were intending to see General Arnold—you were found going south on the post road towards Tarrytown?"

"As I explained earlier to Colonel Jameson, I was going back to take the inner road. I had been told that there were Cowboys out ahead on the post road."

"Who told you?"

"A small boy I met on the road."

"But you ran into our volunteers instead?"

"It seems so. However, I believed that Colonel Jameson would know of me—was indeed expecting me."

"The volunteers had a different story."

I did not reply.

"Then, sir, will you tell me where you reside?"

"Philadelphia. But business brought me to New York."

"You had business dealings with General Arnold?"

"Yes."

"Concerning what?"

"I can only discuss that with General Arnold's consent."

Jameson had left the room, and I was alone with Tallmadge. I took him to be several years younger than myself, but no tyro. Before beginning the interrogation, he had lent me some clothes to wear while mine dried, and this was now our second session of question and answer. Jameson had been present at the first. The questions Tallmadge put to me were direct and proper; his manner was not at all overbearing. I told myself that I should be on guard against the natural friendliness of the man. I asked if I might be allowed to walk around in the room, as I felt chilled. He gave his permission. But he continued to keep his eyes on me as I paced across the room, turned when I reached the wall, and paced back again.

It must have been well past midnight, but no longer having a watch I was not sure how late it was. An oil lamp stood on the mantelpiece, the yellowy light burning unsteadily—brighter, then dimmer. After the first questioning with Tallmadge and Jameson I had been put for an interval in a back room, from which I could hear not so much words as tones—the firmer voice, which was Tallmadge's, and the now and then louder, deeper, and somewhat protesting voice of Jameson. It was not quite an argument—Jameson was superior in rank—but clearly a discussion in which the parties did not agree. I heard Allen summoned; and then his voice came through more sharply: "Yes, sir. I will set off again at once, sir." When I was called in again, Allen had left, and Jameson stayed only a moment or so, appraising me, before he also withdrew.

I paced half a dozen times back and forth across the room. I thought the time had come to test a suspicion I had formed. This was that Tallmadge had had me brought back here, had convinced Jameson that it had been foolish to send me direct to Robinson's and the General. I asked Tallmadge, "If it is not possible for me to be taken to General Arnold, may I at least let him know that I am here?"

Tallmadge glanced reluctantly at the door through which Colonel Jameson had departed as he said, "Yes, Mr. Anderson. That is now being done."

I thought it worthwhile to exploit further what seemed to be a zone of disagreement between the two Americans. I said, "Since the papers I had with me were for General Arnold, and patently of value, I hope they are being sent to him, too. There should be no delay."

Tallmadge said nothing in reply to this. The silence caused my heart to sink. I turned towards the fireplace, with my back to Tallmadge, so that he should not see my face and read there the message of imposture, if this had not been visible to him already. When I asked myself what I would have done with the papers, in his place, there was no equivocation in my mind; I would have sent them at once to General Washington. Tallmadge would do that, must do that. In that way he would make up for his failure to convince Jameson that Allen should not go to Robinson's. Why forewarn Arnold if it was a plot that had been uncovered?

Tallmadge walked round and leaned against the mantelpiece; he looked me in the eye and smiled slightly as he spoke: "Is there anything else you care to tell me that might improve our understanding?"

"I believe I have told you all I can."

For the moment, at any rate! But even as I said those words, I knew that there would be more to tell. Tallmadge would probably be on hand. Much of the time we live with little apprehension of what will be. Memories of the past crowd about us and the present creates an immediate, preoccupying bustle. But now the future rushed in upon me like a black night wind.

I was placed once again in the back room. A blanket was sent in, and the door locked and bolted. A guard was posted outside the window. Major Tallmadge was doing his job. This was, in a way, a relief. For a few hours I slept.

It was still dark when I was awakened and told to prepare myself for a ride. This time my escort was a sergeant and half a dozen men. My importance had been enhanced. For a mile or so it was the same road I had taken northward with Allen twelve hours before, but now, at the first junction, we took the right fork: our course was northeast rather than northwest. I gathered that I was not going to Robinson's, at least not this night. We were on the road to Bedford and Pound Ridge. When I asked about our destination, the Sergeant answered gruffly, as if to say that this was the only question he would answer: "We're going to Colonel Sheldon's, at South Salem."

My clothes had been returned, grubby and not yet quite dry. I was glad of my cape, which worn over Smith's jacket kept out the night chill. It was about an hour before dawn. This riding by dark around the countryside, heading God knows where, seemed to be becoming a habit with me—last night with Smith; the previous night with Arnold; tonight, the longest yet, with Allen first, and then this sergeant. Was it a sort of doom, a fate to which I was henceforth seized? Jack André, for eternity, to ride through the night along the roads of Westchester, tormented by hobgoblins and evil spirits, beset by Cowboys and Skinners! The rain had ceased, which was a mercy, and a few stars were to be seen in patches overhead. Sometimes the stars make me feel small and unimportant. Sometimes they give me a splendid feeling of good fortune—how lucky I am to have been born, to partake of the wonders of creation. Now, as the stars began to fade with the approach of dawn, their milky clusters were a rueful reminder of a childhood belief in heaven, where the angels had their home. Kneeling at the side of my bed, I would pray to my guardian angel: Look after my parents, my brother and sisters. Most of all, look after me. But the angel had departed, had winged away, perhaps to watch over a more deserving soul.

Riding with Allen towards Robinson's, I had been able to doze now and then in the saddle. On this ride I could not. The track was muddy, sometimes slippery. The horses stepped cautiously. My nerves jangled, and I felt itchy and irritable. I rubbed the stubble on my chin. I would have liked a bath and a clean bed and a

long uninterrupted sleep between linen sheets. Goddamn this idiotic conflict! Goddamn Arnold and Smith
—and, particularly, Goddamn Livingston and his
clever notion of firing on the *Vulture*. Oh, for some
magic or sleight of hand. I had seen Isaac Levy perform
his vanishing act at Roubalet's Tavern two weeks ago,
and that was what I needed now. Hey presto!—suddenly to reappear at headquarters on Broadway. It
would surprise Sir Henry.

If wishing were enough, I would have been there.
But the shapes and sounds of men on horseback re-
asserted themselves around me. I began to tire of this
unsuccessful man of commerce, John Anderson. The
ride was prolonged. I thought of Honora and Anna in
that charming dressing room: the gossip of the cathedral close; a book, *The Life of Colonel Jacque* by
Defoe, found at Johnson's shop; making toast at the
fire, and drinking tea; Mrs. Seward knocking at the
door and saying it would soon be time for evensong;
the Canon's springers barking in the side yard as he
returned from his walk around Stowe Pool. A world
away—had it ever existed? The past is delectable when
one can cling to particular fragments of it and enjoy
them once again. But when those fragments threaten to
vanish in the face of the present moment; when one's
own history seems insubstantial; when all is thin and
frail and on the edge of extinction . . . If I ramble now,
it reflects the way my mind meandered moodily then.

It was near eight, I believe, when we came down
through the wooded hills of Pound Ridge to the village
of South Salem. White mist was rising like steam from
thick stands of trees. One of the men in my escort was
whistling a jig, a tune I had heard before; somebody,
at any rate, was happy that our journey was over. The

headquarters of the Second Connecticut Regiment of Light Infantry, Colonel Sheldon commanding, was nicely situated in a comfortable farmhouse flanked by a pair of tall elms. Barn, fences, and fields were in remarkably good order. I was also pleased that the ride was at an end. It was here that Sergeant Dean handed me over with due formality to you, King, at the same time as he delivered to you a letter from Major Tallmadge. And as you and Tallmadge have accompanied me on my travels in the days since then, you may not have realized how grateful I have been for your company. I have begun to feel that we are a small band of brothers, with a comradeship that rises above the petty squabbles of trade and tax and government that divide our countries. Oh yes, I now admit yours as a country, too. Do you know, I thought you were an Irishman when I saw you first, King, with your ginger hair and small stature. If I had come across you at a race meeting about to ride, I would have wagered on your horse.

However, at Sheldon's that morning, when you took me upstairs and left me in a bedroom smaller than this, and locked me in, saying you would return in a few minutes, no doubt after reading what Tallmadge had had to say about me, I made an attempt to pull myself together. Feelings of comradeship were not uppermost at that moment. Feelings of self-preservation were. I was recollecting all I knew about John Anderson and trying to hammer into a more fortunate shape his sorry tale. I was telling myself no battle is lost until at the end one has seen who is left in charge of the field. And then, King, you returned and spoiled it all! Do you know how you did that? I can see you at this minute coming in through the door—the latch lifted, the door swung open, and then you stood and gazed at me with such frank curiosity and pity. As if to say, You poor fellow, what a state you look to be in! You said, "The barber is coming up to dress me. Would you like him to attend to you while he is here?"

This gesture of gentlemanly courtesy caught me by surprise. Indeed, it moved me. I had trouble preventing myself from showing it. Tears, my dear King, tears welled up. Of course I know, as presumably you do, how to exact information from prisoners with sudden alternations of intimidation and affected friendliness. But there had been little intimidation to date, after the Skinners had done with me, merely a coolness and not unnatural severity of manner; and this act of yours seemed spontaneous, to be responded to in like manner. It was for this reason that I so openly expressed my appreciation—and felt even more obliged when, in answer to my suggestion that I take to the bed while my clothes were washed, you proposed that I borrow some of yours.

It is some time since I have given any thought to how you Rebels arrange your toilet. Despite living among you in Lancaster, part of my mind has continued to insist that you are all peasant farmers or noble savages, unconcerned with these things. Yet the barber of the Second Connecticut did not seem very different from those members of his profession we had at headquarters in New York. Most barbers have a grand sense of their own skills, whether in shaving or hacking off wounded limbs. The work of a butcher or thatcher requires just as much art, if you ask me. But, at least in our forces, with fashion demanding that officers have their hair properly arranged and powdered for morning parade, the elevated ideas of the

barbering fraternity have been sustained, if not rein-
forced. Your barber was like nearly every other barber
I have encountered in that he loved to talk. While he
worked on me, I had little choice but to listen.

"If you don't mind my remarking on it, sir," he
commenced, "your hair's a mess." He was a portly,
middle-aged figure, bald, in a once-white apron. He
untied the ribbon which held my hair together at the
nape and brushed out the last powder remaining in it.
He went on: "Looks to me as though you've spent
the last week or so in the woods. Still, I think we've
got it before things start growing up here. I don't
know who your regular dresser might be, sir, but I
trust he'll approve of whatever expedients I can apply."

He was happy with the challenge, it appeared, and
satisfied with the opportunity for an uninterrupted
soliloquy. In its opening stages I let it wash over me:
the inflated price of ribbon; the advantages of Hodg-
kinson's Improved Powder; the merits of domestic
wigs, made in Boston, and now considered by many
senior officers to be superior to the imported variety;
the certainty that the Continental gentlemen now had
hair more finely turned out than the officers of the
Crown (if only the conflict could have been confined
to a competition of this kind!). On any other occasion
I would have relaxed under this benign flow of incon-
sequence and even enjoyed the sensations aroused by
brush and comb. But as the soap was lathered on and
the razor was stropped, I began to feel very much on
edge. I was sure that I was visibly shaking. My nerves
were exposed, and surely were liable to be sliced off,
like the bristles on my chin under the creamy cover of
soap.

"Steady on, sir, or I'll do you a damage."

King—you were watching me, I know. You were thinking about the traces of powder in my hair and what that portended. Tallmadge had had the same look earlier as he watched me pace around the room at North Castle, the pleased look of someone whose suspicions are becoming a conviction. I knew it as I paced, and by then of course it was too late to change my gait to something more civilian, less that of one who has been bred to arms. I was aware of you, King, and I was aware of *everything* around me: the bubbles in the froth of soap; the stroke of the towel wiping it away; the gleaming steel of the razor which lay on a side table; the grain of the wood—pine; the light reflected from the steel; the branches of the elm moving just outside the window; a succession of gusts of warm morning air, each separate, particular, yet intermingled and interdependent. And sounds—a branch rubbing against another branch, the barber wiping his hands, a bird, and voices in the yard below. One voice could be recognized.

"It's Major Tallmadge," I heard you say. "He must have arrived this moment."

After an instant of agitation, the fact was calming. Here was someone I already knew, a man who could be trusted. That he was a Rebel officer no longer seemed to matter. I stretched out on the bed while the barber proceeded to shave you, King. I closed my eyes. I jogged and swayed on horseback again, the dirt road beneath with its stones and declivities, my view of it ahead parted by the ears and mane of Jupiter, and to each side the massed green leaves shot through by sunlight, yellow blobs in pools of green, blurs of light. A rough log bridge over a stream. A clump of trees throwing deep shadows across the road. Across the bridge, I rode up the slope to the top of a little hill which afforded a prospect of Tarrytown.

With my eyelids lifted, I could see you putting your jacket on. The barber had gone. It was time for break fast. And I ate with real appetite. The Gilbert farm had clearly come provided with livestock. There was no shortage of hard-boiled eggs, bacon, milk, cheese, and bread. Perhaps it was the food, the short rest, or even the attentions of the barber, but my spirits were suddenly high. Not happy—by no means joyful—but high with a sense of a difficult corner having been turned, a knowledge that there was no longer any need for difficult decisions to be made. I was pleased, in a vicarious way, for Tallmadge and you, King; it would be a great success for you, perhaps the most noteworthy thing that had happened in some time. *I* could take credit for that. And I arrived at these feelings, paradoxically, by imagining the worst.

Tallmadge soon confirmed these imaginings. He came in, mopping sweat from his face with a large handkerchief. He said cheerfully, "You look restored, Mr. Anderson."

"I'm obliged for your courtesy," I said. "Lieutenant King is taking excellent care of me."

You, King, said, "Mr. Anderson has not even uttered a word of protest about not being able to continue his journey to Robinson's"—as if your colleague should have this information about my state of well-being before he had a chance to say more.

Tallmadge took this in. But it did not puzzle him; it seemed on the contrary to make it simpler for him to continue. He said to me: "You asked me last night about the papers you were carrying. I can tell you now what has happened to them. I came here in company

with Captain Hoogland. He has just left to take the
papers to the General at Danbury."

The General. For a fraction of time I felt an up-
heaval—the confident calm of despair became the
turbulence of hope. And then calm again, as it
occurred to me that Arnold would not be at Danbury.
The general referred to was *the* General. It had to be.
I said, "You have sent them to General Washington?"

"We have, sir." The "we" perhaps generously included Colonel Jameson, who if he had had his way
would have compounded the fault already committed
and sent them to Arnold. Tallmadge added, "It will
therefore be necessary to keep you here at Salem until
we hear from his Excellency."

"I understand."

Washington, not Arnold, would determine my
condition.

It was kind of you, King, to propose at that moment
a turn in the yard. However much I had expected this
message from Tallmadge, the shock of actually receiving it was considerable. I needed the air and the sunlight. A bell was ringing in the village. It was Sunday
—I had forgotten. Church. Hymns. He who would
valiant be. And he who would be truthful, while
trying to save his own scalp, if both actions could con-
currently be performed. Something had to be rescued
from this pickle, if only my own reputation as a man
of honour. Perhaps, if the truth could be presented in
the right way . . . You walked with me back and
forth across the yard. The right-hand door of the barn
was sagging. Guards were posted at the entrance to
the yard. A whiff of manure came to me. Back and
forth. Shadow of a bird sweeping over the yard. I have

never liked the idea of keeping birds caged and forcing them to sing. Even as a prisoner, I felt bound to act like a free man. So *I* took the decision; it did not take me.

My requests were met with immediate attention. Tallmadge himself brought up to the bedroom, soon after I returned to it, pen, ink, and paper. The small pine table, placed under the window, would serve as a writing desk. I waited until you, King, had gone to stand guard outside the door before I took up the pen. We writers prefer privacy if we can get it. And then I sought words. Usually I have a facile way with them, but on this occasion they were slow to come. I had ceased to be apprehensive about Arnold's safety. He should have had at least a twelve-hour notice, giving him enough time to decide what to do. This was not to say that I had ceased to blame him, for in the back of my mind I damned him for not making a better, surer plan and for not forcing Smith to take me back by water. But now I wanted to be free of John Anderson and his failed mission, even if this meant that, by resuming my own name and identity, I was freeing myself from the last protection the imposture gave me. However, I was not seeking security. I was simply hoping to vindicate the character of John André and the small amount of fame that might soon be all that was left of him.

It was afternoon before the pen—dipped frequently but profitlessly in the ink well—began to shape the formal words I addressed to General Washington. I wrote that whatever I had said to date had been in an attempt (I thought justifiable) to extricate myself. I was too little accustomed to duplicity to have succeeded. I begged his Excellency to understand that what induced me to take this step of addressing him was not apprehension for my own safety. It was rather to rescue myself from the imputation of having assumed a false character for treacherous purposes or self-interest. I spoke now in order to vindicate my fame and not to solicit security. The person in his possession was Major John André, Adjutant General to the British Army.

I paused and looked out at the yard through the window. Some horses were being led towards the stable. What I had written so far would do; it was truthful, if slightly coloured by a need to reacquire self-esteem. There remained the task of explaining, up to a point, what John Anderson had been doing. To influence a commander in the army of one's adversary was (I wrote) an advantage one might take in war. A correspondence for this purpose I had conducted, confidentially, on behalf of his Excellency Sir Henry Clinton. To favour it, I agreed to meet—on ground that was not within the posts of either army—a person who was to give me intelligence. I came upriver in the man-of-war *Vulture* for this purpose. I was fetched by a boat from the shore. While I was on land, I was told that the approach of day would prevent my return and that I must be concealed until the next night. I was in my regimental uniform and had fairly risked my person. (In other words, I had not come ashore in disguise. I had no intention of being a spy.)

Against my stipulation, and without my knowledge beforehand, I was conducted within one of the American posts. I hoped his Excellency would conceive my feelings as I realized this, and would imagine how I was affected by a refusal to bring me back the next night in the same way as I had been brought.

(I had had no choice. Surely Washington would see that.)

Thus become a prisoner, I had to arrange my escape. I quitted my uniform and was passed another way in the night without the American posts to neutral ground. I was told that I was beyond all armed parties and left to make my way to New York. I was taken at Tarrytown by some volunteers. And thus, as I had the honour to relate, was I betrayed into the vile condition of an enemy in disguise within the American posts.

(That was the easiest, if slowest, part of the letter to write. I now had to face the logic of the situation. "The vile condition," however unwitting had been my intention to fall into it, was that of a spy. Spies met with but one end. Death was bad enough, but a shameful death, which would cling to me past the grave! I felt it loom up monstrously and reach out to envelop me. When I took up the pen again, it was as if it might be a lance with which to prod the fear away.)

Now, having avowed myself a British officer, it only remained to make one request of his Excellency. This was that in any rigour policy might dictate, a decency of conduct towards me might demonstrate that, however unfortunate, I was not to be branded with anything dishonourable. My only motive was the service of my King, and I was involuntarily an impostor.

I closed by asking permission to write an open letter to Sir Henry Clinton, and also to a friend who would send me clothes and linen. And I mentioned some American officers, held captive by us at Charleston, who—while under parole—had engaged in a conspiracy against us. Their position was not exactly similar to mine, but they might, conceivably, be exchanged for me, or might be affected, in regard to the treatment they received, by the treatment I was to receive.

(I didn't mean this to sound like a threat. But I could conceive Sir Henry in a rage: If they touch a hair of John André's head, I'll hang fifty American prisoners!)

I had the honour to be, with great respect, his Excellency's most obedient and most humble servant.

Tallmadge read the letter, which I put in his hands. He said, "I was pretty sure, sir, that you were a British officer. Lieutenant King agreed with me. But we did not suspect your importance." He began to fold the letter. "You were after a big fish."

"It seemed possible."

"And very nearly was."

He looked at me directly, and there was a note in his voice, almost sympathetic, as if he were aware that his sense of success had to be matched by my sense of failure. Then he said, "Well, you'll excuse me, Major André, and I will see your letter dispatched at once to General Washington."

It was something to hear my own name spoken again.

We have ten minutes before the proceedings, you say? In that case, I would like to take a turn first in the garden here, Mr. King, if that is agreeable with you. It is not quite as picturesque as the yard at the Gilbert farm. I think that for some reason I prefer the country east of Hudson's, yes, even the landscape just north of Tarrytown, to this on the west of the river. A walk outside may be calming for the spirits. This will be my first experience of military justice, of being, that is, on the end that receives. I have taken part in courts-martial. A few years ago I was on a board asked to determine a dispute between two officers, a lieutenant colonel and a lieutenant, who were, as it happened, related—uncle and nephew, I believe. The young man had been publicly reprimanded by his uncle, and when he answered back, he was put under arrest. However, it was established, in his defense, that his uncle, the Colonel, repaired too often to the bottle. We found for the young man. The Colonel's punishment, not surprisingly, was set aside not long after. On other occasions, I was on the courts of two privates tried for desertion—one was hanged, one had his sentence respited; I forget the difference of merit in their cases. The relatively greater harshness of one sentence may have been because we were about to engage an American force and needed every man. Or it may have arisen from the whim of a different commanding officer. We have not been noted for consistency in this conflict, unless it is the consistency of hesitation. We call you rebels; but rebels should be shot, and invariably we have treated your men when captured as prisoners of war. Our motives for this may have resided in the hope of bringing our captives round to their true allegiance, or in the fear of retaliation against men of ours taken prisoner by you. I have not shared this latter apprehension. I have had the impression our troops were welcomed when taken prisoner for the hard money they were able to spend in local markets. Such was our belief concerning General Burgoyne's men—that you have held on to them, despite the Convention that was signed on their surrender, for commercial reasons. Others have said that you have kept them because you realized that sending them back to England on parole (with an undertaking not to serve here again) would nevertheless release other troops for service in North America. Policy frequently takes precedence over a strict adherence to the rules of war; now and again policy demands such an adherence. As for custom and practice, they are sometimes the parents of error—I am thinking of our habit of going into winter quarters, as Sir William Howe had us go in '76–'77. Thus we lost our best chance of destroying General Washington and his army.

Well, I see a small detachment has arrived to march me to the church. I will tell you what transpires, King —whether they decide to baptize me or bury me. Don't look so glum!

You will undoubtedly hear of it from Major Tallmadge, Mr. King. The Major was in attendance, although not a member of the Board. On that there was no one below the rank of brigadier general; there were eight of those, and six major generals. I would say this display of generalcy was meant to demonstrate to the world that I was being dealt with by men of experience and without obvious partiality. But I admit to being impressed. And, as you can see, also a trifle shattered by the whole affair—I would rather face a cavalry charge. They have said that they will make their report this afternoon and I will be given cognizance of its findings. So it is not long to wait. Perhaps I shall attempt to draw the scene for you and keep my mind from dwelling on the likely verdict. You know the church, I assume. It is an appropriate place in many respects. Several of the pews at the front had been moved back to make a space, and in this was placed a long table—or was it two tables?—at which the Board sat, as in a painting of the Last Supper. I was brought before them, to stand, and eventually to sit on the foremost pew, accompanied by Tallmadge and some soldiery. But no Dutch dominie said prayers. I wonder if my Geneva childhood predestined me to this. A gentleman whom I understood to be the Judge Advocate General read out to me the names of the officers of the Board, and as each of the names was spoken, the bearer gave a slight acknowledgement: a nod, a grimace, a slight bow, even. Major General Nathaniel Greene, the Board president—is it true he was a blacksmith once?—certainly bluff and no nonsense; but very correct and apparently familiar with the law; square-faced, with regular, trustworthy features. The other major generals were Lord Stirling, St. Clair, the Marquis de Lafayette, your Howe, and the Baron von Steuben; in other words, they included two Scotsmen, one Frenchman, one Prussian; one claimant to an earldom, *un Marquis*, *ein Baron*, and one blacksmith. The eldest was Stirling, whom I judged to be in his mid-fifties, while the youngest was Lafayette, a stripling of—what?—twenty-three? I was indeed glad to see that General Wayne, the tanner, was not of their number. He might have exacted immediate revenge for my *Cow-Chase*.

Have you ever sat with fourteen pairs of eyes looking at you? The assembled, accumulated experience of fourteen men aimed at you, taking you in, *judging* you. This is the Enemy, they were clearly thinking; this is the King's man. And so I was. Poor George, my monarch, to have so frail a reed as his representative in Tappan today! But I was firm in my resolve—I would do my best to the last. All those eyes were upon me as a letter from his Excellency General Washington was read aloud by the Advocate General. It said that I, Adjutant General to the British Army, was to be examined by the Board; that I had come within your lines by night, on an interview with Major General Arnold, in an assumed character; and that I was taken captive within your lines, in a disguised habit, with a pass in a feigned name, and with certain papers found upon me. My examination was to be careful but a report produced as speedily as possible; the Board was to give its precise opinion of my case, together with its view of the light in which I should be considered and the punishment that should be inflicted.

I was asked to stand again. General Greene said that I was to be asked various questions, and that I should feel perfectly at liberty to answer them as I chose. I was to take my time for recollection, and weigh well what I would say. I bowed in reply.

I was asked if I were Major John André.

I was.

I was asked if I were Adjutant General to the British forces.

I was. (I declined to qualify my post with the term "acting.")

I was asked if I had any objection to any of the members of the Board.

I had not.

I then heard read out the letter that I had written to General Washington from Salem last Sunday. This took several minutes. The multitude of eyes had by now ceased to examine me. I think the owners of them began to be uneasy to meet mine. But I did encounter the passing glance of one—Brigadier General Parsons, I believe; a disgruntled-looking man. Perhaps there were other reasons, other than compassion for me, for his not wanting to be there. (Sir Henry had suggested that General Parsons might be ripe for a correspondence with us, too.) When the end of the lettter had been reached I was asked if I had written it, and I acknowledged that I had. I was then asked to confirm several points of the letter: how I came on shore and precisely where (from the *Vulture*, sloop-of-war; to land under Haverstraw mountain); whether the boat I came in carried a flag of truce (no); and what I wore (a cape over my regimentals). As to what I had done there, I confirmed again that I had met and had an interview with a person on shore. I was asked his name and said that I wished not to mention the names of anyone other than myself. General Greene agreed, but asked, "When you came on shore and met this— person, did you consider yourself acting as a private individual or as a British officer?"

I replied: "I wore my uniform, and considered myself as what indeed I was, a British officer."

And then, item by item, the rest. There was nothing to deny. There were a few points to be emphasized, but they underlined my bad fortune rather than the justice or propriety of my actions. For example, my surprise at finding myself conducted behind the American lines. Or the disagreeable sensations I had felt on learning that I was not to return to the *Vulture* by boat, and had to don other clothing. When the president mentioned Smith's house, I interrupted him: "Sir, I said a house, but I did not say whose house."

"True," said General Greene.

It was pointed out that I wore the jacket of another person, and I agreed it was not my regimental coat. We went through, once more, the manner in which I was taken near Tarrytown while on the way to the

White Plains and New York. Then the papers were shown the Board and held up before me. I was asked if these were the same papers that had been found on me, all concealed in my boot save for the pass which I had eventually shown. I agreed that they were the same papers. The pass was in the name of John Anderson, a name I acknowledged I had assumed. The artillery orders of September 5. The estimate of forces at West Point and its dependencies. The ordnance return at West Point, and remarks on works. The matters laid before a Council of War by General Washington on September 6. General Greene asked: "Who gave these papers to you?"

I replied, "I feel unable to say."

"You do not know?"

"I will not divulge any names."

I was then interrogated about the notion that I could have come on shore under a flag of truce. I said that it was of course impossible that I had landed under such a sanction—that if I had done so, then naturally I might have returned under such a flag.

I was then asked if I had anything further to say about the facts that had been so far established. I answered that I agreed they were true, and that I left them to operate with the Board. General Greene asked the other members if they saw any need to call further witnesses and remarked that for himself he saw no need; the others agreed with him. General Greene said: "Sit down for the moment, Major André." He sounded almost paternal. He rose and went to the far end of the church with the Advocate General—Mr. Lawrence, I think he is—where they talked. Next to the pulpit, to the right of where I was placed, a small board showed the numbers of the hymns that had been sung at the last service, perhaps last Sunday. I wondered what they had been. Did the burghers of Tappan know our Bunyan?

> *Since, Lord, thou dost defend*
> *Us with thy Spirit,*
> *We know we at the end*
> *Shall life inherit.*

Though I have always felt the hereafter was a risky exchange for the present one.

General Greene returned to his seat, and I stood again. He said, "Major André, there are several letters now to be considered by the Board. We have been discussing whether they should be read to the Board alone or in your presence. We have determined that you will be allowed to hear them."

"I am obliged, sir."

The Judge Advocate then read a letter from General Arnold. It was dated September 25—Monday, four days ago—and was written on board the *Vulture*. From my point of view, it was fortunate that I had not been kept in suspense for long about Arnold's escape. Tallmadge had told me of it when we arrived at West Point on Tuesday, perhaps in the hope that my reaction to the news of my accomplice's flight would contribute information of benefit to the American cause. As it was, I now listened calmly to Arnold's words, no doubt written at the same table where I had penned to him the calculated letter of protest about the *Vulture*'s boat being fired on from the shore while answering a flag. He was there, and I was here. He wrote, among other things: "I have ever acted from a principle of love to my country." He asked that his wife be allowed to go to Philadelphia or join him on the *Vulture*. He held as blameless several officers on his staff and declared that Joshua Hett Smith was ignorant of the nature of the transactions he, Arnold, had been conducting.

Mr. Lawrence paused and glanced at General Greene. General Greene gave a quick look along the tables in both directions, as if for comment. Lafayette was giving Steuben a wry smile. No one spoke. Greene said, "And the next piece of correspondence?"

The Judge Advocate said, "This is from Colonel Robinson, also September 25, on the *Vulture* off Sinsink. To his Excellency General Washington." Robinson staunchly claimed that I had gone up with a flag at the request of General Arnold for public business with him. Under those circumstances, there was of course no reason for detaining me. Every step I had taken was by the advice and direction of General Arnold, even that of adopting a feigned name, and therefore I was not liable to censure for those acts. Robinson closed with a reminder to General Washington of their former acquaintance. Hadn't they been youthful friends in Virginia?

Mr. Lawrence put down Robinson's letter and picked up another. This, he said, was from General Sir Henry Clinton to General Washington. From New York, September 26. It declared that I had been detained while under General Arnold's passports, and that a flag of truce had been sent for my return, and passports dispatched from New York. Sir Henry had no doubts, therefore, that I would be given permission to return to his orders in New York. None of the Board smiled at this, though I would not have blaméd any who had done so.

General Greene at this point had a word with the

two members sitting on either side of him, General
St. Clair and Lord Stirling (I shall use his title even if
the House of Lords has rejected his claim to it).
Greene's gaze skimmed over me as he turned from one
general to the other. There was a silence then for some
moments. Mr. Lawrence scribbled a few notes. Fourteen gloomy men sat looking at the tabletops in front
of them or, over my head, at the sunlight falling in
bright shafts into the church. At last General Greene
spoke: "Major André."

"Sir." I stood up, to attention. It would have been
pleasant to have been wearing my regimentals now.

"You are remanded into custody while the Board
considers the results of this examination. I will say no
more at present, other than to tell you that we are
sensible of the candour and forthrightness which you
have displayed at these proceedings."

And that was it—apart from a comment from Mr.
Lawrence that I would receive a copy of the Board's
report as soon as it was made. I do not imagine they
will take very long, do you? I feel the way one sometimes does after a crucial conference or even a dinner
engagement, that there were bright and important
things I neglected to say. Never mind! I should like to
write, in a little while, if it is permitted, to my commander Sir Henry in New York. He must be assured
that it was through no fault of his that things mis-
carried. And a sudden thought intrudes: how well
organized we are, how punctilious in terms of ceremony and protocol, which frame our conflicts. Yet
for many the inescapable upshot of the whole business
is death. Whether of hundreds in battle or of a single
man brought to trial. Do our conventions make the

underlying savagery any the less? Perhaps. I cannot help thinking that the style with which any act is performed is part of the nature of the act, and will be, as it were, part of the judgement.

Let me show you, King, my letter to Sir Henry Clinton. I have left it unsealed, since I assume that you will want to show it to Major Tallmadge when asking permission for me to have it sent to New York. It was only a shade less difficult to write than my letter to General Washington last Sunday. Sir Henry has been my mentor, and it is a role that he does not easily adopt. He is a complicated man, happy when playing his violin or in domestic circumstances with Mrs. Baddeley, but otherwise the uneasiest of senior officers —he can be a real porcupine. The unease communicates itself. Most people feel it, though my relations with him were thankfully free of it. On one occasion, however, even I aroused his distrust, his feeling of being opposed and disliked (feelings, you might think, that should be quite unnecessary in the supreme commander on these shores, but are, I can assure you, most aggravatingly and destructively common with him). The occasion was two months ago—I mentioned it to Tallmadge yesterday. We were on shipboard, going to Huntington Bay, when Sir Henry abruptly imagined that someone had tried to poison him by putting arsenic in the wine. Delancey was also sick, and so was Beckwith, but I—though I had drunk of the wine, too—had no ill effects, a fact which bothered Sir Henry. As the fount of the conspiracy, Governor Livingston of New Jersey was suspected by Sir Henry —he had treated the good Governor with scorn a year before. These Livingstons have a long arm! One element in the case that aroused suspicion in the minds of Sir Henry's staff was that the bottle, still holding a glass or two of wine, disappeared in the night, though Sir Henry said that he had kept it behind his pillow. The person most likely to have dropped it into the Sound was Sir Henry himself. He, Delancey, and Beckwith, moreover, had all eaten the same shellfish as Sir Henry, while I had not.

I have tried in my letter, as you will see, to set his mind at rest in regard to my condition here. I have assured him of my most certain realization that the mistakes I have made were not the result of any orders he had given me—rather, that they arose from my acting contrary to his instructions. I also want him to know that I am perfectly tranquil in mind and pre- pared for any fate to which—through honest zeal for the King's service—I may be committed. I have thanked him for his concern for my career. I have reminded him of my mother and sisters, whose income from my father's estate has been affected by the loss of Grenada to the French, and to whom the value of my commission will be a matter of interest. It would be beneficial for them if my field rank of major could be confirmed by Whitehall, for the rank, when my com- mission is sold, will bring almost twice as much as a captaincy. I conclude by telling Sir Henry of the courtesy with which I am being treated here. It may ease his mind a little at a moment when his hopes have in general taken a great blow.

On Monday at the Gilbert farmhouse, although I knew which day it was, time in other senses seemed to be suspended. Letters and messages had been sent. Various events were proceeding elsewhere. By now

Arnold must have heard that I had been taken. General Washington would soon be returning from his conference with the French. This was the day that we had intended to mount our attack on West Point. The wind was southwesterly, according to the vane in the shape of a bull which pivoted above the ridge of the barn. A perfect wind for the voyage upriver. I wondered whether Sir Henry would still attempt the expedition, but assumed that he would not move, having heard the worst by now or having had nothing confirmed. Caution was his password. Major Tallmadge was obviously speculating along the same lines as myself, although he did not have such close experience of Sir Henry's caution. The papers from my boot had got their message through to him, and he saw the prize we had been after, and which Arnold had meant to render up to us. As the day wore on, Tallmadge more than I continued to fear the assault on West Point; he must have doubted whether the dispatch to warn General Washington had been sent in time. It made him more irritable than I had yet seen him. The shine of his success looked like being a little dulled! By afternoon he had decided to beard me with it. Arnold's "treachery," as Tallmadge termed it, was perfidious. Any victory gained through such means was of less true value, not just in the eyes of military men, but in the view of history.

I begged to differ. I pointed out to him that there were numerous precedents for such action—he had only to look at Roman history. As a teacher, he should recall how frequently generals changed sides, rebelled against their rulers, or returned to their true allegiances, and the destiny of empire was thereby affected. History absolved success of whatever shifts had been practiced to achieve it; it emphasized those factors that had led to failure. Treason was given that name only by those it injured. From our point of view, not only was General Arnold returning to his proper allegiance, but he was doing so in an active way. The capture of West Point by the King's forces would, I believed, shorten the war and save the lives of many men who would otherwise die in battle, siege, and skirmish. (I did not, to be honest, allude to the financial considerations that had attended our arrangements with General Arnold.)

When Tallmadge left me, I fell to daydreaming. I decided that when I quit the military service, I would start a new life as a playwright. I have a distinguished associate in that line of work in General Burgoyne, who is said to be very talented in sketch writing. (Or is it that we share a similar flaw, a similar lack of conviction about which of our talents we should take most seriously?) Do you know the works of George Farquhar, Mr. King? *The Beaux' Stratagem? The Recruiting Officer?* Farquhar was a military man before he turned to the stage; he went recruiting in Lichfield, of all places, and in that fair city his play *The Beaux' Stratagem* is set. It is a piece with plenty of comic disguise and feigned identity. The chief parts are those of Aimwell and Archer, two friends in reduced circumstances who take it in turn to be master and servant. While Aimwell is master, he borrows his elder brother's title of viscount in order to win the fair Dorinda's hand. However, honesty overcomes Aimwell at the last; he tells her the truth and is rewarded with news of his brother's death, so that he is indeed viscount now. It always struck me how little sadness Aimwell demonstrates on hearing this. In *The*

Recruiting Officer it is our heroine Silvia who adopts a feigned character. Out of love for Captain Plume, the recruiting officer, she pretends to be one Jack Wilful, wears man's apparel, and is recruited. In the course of the play Silvia becomes sole heiress to her father's estate, worth about twelve hundred pounds a year, on the sudden death of her brother. How our playwright makes use of these sudden deaths of brothers! Her father, Justice Balance, says, "The strokes of heaven I can bear; but injuries from men are not so easily supported." I played Captain Plume once. It is important in such plays to have several plots going at once, and intermingle them, with plenty of confusion. Throw in a few country people, yokels or thieves, and give them names like Paulding, Williams, and van Wart. What shall we call our play, King— *The Jaeger Jacket*? So far we have not had enough feminine interest. That must be remedied.

I have been thinking of Honora. I gave up wearing the locket only a month ago; I wish I had it now. You know, she married this fellow Edgeworth. He turned up in Lichfield the last Christmas before I obtained my commission, a married man still, though his wife was to die two years or so later. He had married at nineteen, while an undergraduate, and regretted it, I think. But he was an athletic sort, Mr. Edgeworth; had been a great rider in his youth. He was full of talk of inventions and improvements—the sort of man who wants to make things faster and communicate more rapidly with people who live at a distance. One of his inventions was a telegraphy machine to signal the results of a horse race; he used it to send such news from Newmarket to London, and thereby won a large bet. He talked a great deal about a device he had made for more efficiently cutting turnips. On a visit to France he had met Rousseau, which impressed Honora. And to balance these enthusiasms he had large estates in Ireland, which impressed the Sewards and Mr. Sneyd, eventually, as offering Honora a good deal more than talent and promise. For so it came to pass. Richard Edgeworth married Honora a few months after he became a widower. And since then there have been hints in Miss Seward's letters to me that he and his demon interest in progress are wearing Honora out, poor girl. She was ever frail. Two children by now, I believe, and no doubt many successors to the telegraphs and the turnip cutters. Does this seem like jealousy on my part? Does it seem childish that I wanted a knighthood and a brigadiership to make evident to Honora that I had had my successes, too?

I was a long way from success last Monday night, as you know, Mr. King. I was not sleeping when you roused me around midnight and said I must prepare myself to ride. Farewell, Salem. I had taken a liking to Mr. Gilbert's farm in the two days I had been there. In another existence perhaps I shall become an American farmer and raise children by the system of Monsieur Rousseau. I have never planned my life far ahead—no soldier can. But I had begun to think that in my thirties I might settle for matrimony and a child or two. When I was home again, I would accompany my mother, perhaps to Bath this time, and find a young lady of good family in one of the drawing rooms, and stand for Parliament.

Only now it looked as though I would be drowned first. As we stepped out of Mr. Gilbert's, rain was teeming down. Your men did not seem happy at the prospect of a night-long ride in those conditions. I gathered that word from General Washington had been received, and that I was being moved by his orders. Your men were in strength. It seemed that, with each ride I made, the numbers accompanying me increased. This time I had a whole troop of dragoons for escort as we set out northwards. Tallmadge met us at North Salem church and, after talking with you, appeared to direct a change of route. I did not ask where we were going. I was preoccupied with the streams of water that cascaded down my face, fell off my eyebrows, poured off my nose, dropped from my cheeks and chin. My cape and jacket beneath were soon sodden. Thank God, the night was warm. I thought perhaps the new route was chosen because General Washington had decided to meet me in some other place than that first directed; or perhaps there was a desire to confuse the enemy, in the event that word had somehow reached the British lines that I was to be taken along a certain way. The route was changed, but the rain continued, and the rain mattered more. However, once I was thoroughly wet I could get no wetter—there is a consolation in having reached the extremity of a condition: all the apprehensions along the way have been passed; nothing worse can happen, or so it seems at the time. I imagined myself back in Hackney, huddled over the fire in the counting room, writing to Honora.

We arrived at Robinson's just after dawn. The rain had ceased; a grey light suffused the misty air. The low farmhouse stood on a small plateau of fields, orchards, and gardens between a sugar-loaf-shaped hill and the east bank of Hudson's river; the river could just be seen through the trees. It impressed me as an older and less elegant house than Belmont, the main structure a stunted two storeys, to which was attached an addition with dormer windows in the roof. I thus had a chance to inspect the property on behalf of Beverley Robinson and see how General Arnold had been caring for it. Or is this the vainglory of amended recollection? To be honest, I believe I looked forward to getting dry, first of all, and then finding out not about the house but what had happened to its tenants-in-chief— to Arnold—and Peggy!

A new face. Ah yes, Colonel Hamilton. Tallmadge has mentioned you, and in any event, your name is not unfamiliar to us in New York. We have heard of his Excellency General Washington's young aide; those who closely attend one general officer are interested in those who perform a similar task for those who lead the other side. You are obviously of fewer years than me and in rank an even greater success. It sits in my memory that you have had work published by Mr. Rivington, too; *and* you speak French. I wonder if we will have an opportunity for conversation in that tongue. But I gather from the concerned expression in your very blue eyes that you are not here to see me for the sake of pleasantries. If it is about the report of the Board of Officers affecting me, it may be easier for you to allow me to read it. My object is not to cause anyone any needless pain.

Well, it is not a lengthy work. I thank you for it. It will not expand by much the sorrows of Jack André, if they ever come to be written. It is as I expected. I am found to have come on shore for an interview with General Arnold in a private and secret manner; to have changed my dress within your lines and then, under a feigned name and in a disguised habit, to have passed your works at Stony and Verplanck's points; to have been taken at Tarrytown, still in a disguised habit, on the way to New York; and to have had then in my possession several papers which contained intelligence for the enemy. The Board has maturely considered these facts. (Would they consider them in any other fashion—immaturely, for instance!) The Board therefore reports to his Excellency General Washington that Major André, Adjutant General to the British Army, ought to be considered as a spy from the enemy, and that, agreeable to the law and usage of nations, he ought to suffer death.

I had not expected anything else, you know, but of course I retained a frail and very slender hope that for some reason Major General Greene and the Board would report otherwise. "Oh, he's a pleasant, harmless fellow—his silly plan didn't work—send him back to New York by the first chaise."

But this is it. He ought to suffer death. I think that if I had been on the Board I would have agreed to that.

At this moment I am feeling strong. I hope I can keep it up.

TAPPAN

Saturday, September 30

1780

Thank you for asking, Tallmadge—I had a good night. I slept the sleep of the innocent or just. Or the sleep of those who are beyond worry. It is a regular life here at Tappan, no excuses for merrymaking and carousals, and no aching head in the morning from being too late at the King's Arms the night before. I could grow to like it. Even this matter of always having company, one of your officers always with me, is not so irksome as I might have imagined; we do not impinge upon one another; we dwell mostly in our own thoughts. And now you have brought me a journal, last week's issue of *Rivington's*. Your intelligence service in New York is working well! I'll trust you will excuse my author's indulgent feelings while I dote on my words in print. Or should I say my mock-heroics? Canto Three, *The Cow-Chase*, by J. André. Chevy Chase came to mind when I heard of General Wayne's most recent exploit, his expedition to New Jersey to take cattle and forage, and his repulse by Loyalists. I thought it an episode worthy of being immemorialized.

O curs'd rebellion! these are thine;
Thine are these tales of woe!

[*141*]

Major André

Shall at thy dire insatiate shrine
Blood never cease to flow?

And here I have a nymph come forth to implore
General Wayne to stop his men cutting down trees.
She is abducted by the General, who in civilian life,
as you probably know, was in the leather business.

> *Great Wayne, by soft compassion sway'd,*
> *To no enquiry stoops;*
> *But takes the fair afflicted maid*
> *Right into Yan Van Poop's.*

> *So Roman Anthony, they say,*
> *Disgrac'd th' imperial banner,*
> *And for a gypsy lost the day;*
> *Like Anthony the tanner.*

> *The Hamadryad had but half*
> *Receiv'd redress from Wayne,*
> *When drums and colours, cow and calf,*
> *Came down the road amain.*

I admire a few things still. "Receiv'd redress"—that's
nice, one of the pleasures of writing verse when
alliteration and meaning and wit fall neatly into place.
The rest, well, is trivial, though I hope it amuses. I
would give a great deal to have the opinion of General
Wayne. Now the hero of my epic has the material
for a counterattack, though I don't know if he has any
talent for versifying. Still, I'll take my chances and
grant him all rights in the matter: *The Adjutant
General.* Or, *The Deputy Adjutant General.* It would
have been good to know whether or not Lord
Amherst, our Commander in Britain, would have confirmed me in the office.

September 30

I see the weather is unsettled once again—grey and damp and warm. Go on, assure me like a native that it will "burn off"! I think I continue to have wet patches under the skin from our ride from Salem to Robinson's last Tuesday. And I am glad it was there that I was taken, a small enough house for all of us who were suddenly in it, a house in which it would have been hard to keep a secret for very long, I'd have thought—despite Arnold's success at just that. As it was, you wanted to find out what had happened as much as I did. Certainly everyone seemed intent on abusing Arnold's aides, Franks and Varick, for their slowness and lack of perception. I don't blame them for defending themselves, even in front of me. What I still don't understand is why Jameson's messenger took so long to reach Robinson's. The intrepid Lieutenant Allen. Did he deliberately delay, realizing the indiscretion of the mission on which Jameson had sent him? This story about falling from his horse—did you believe it? In the event, he got to Robinson's early on Monday morning and Arnold received the dispatch from Jameson only an hour before General Washington arrived from his meeting with Rochambeau. I can imagine Arnold opening the letter and reading the lines "A gentleman calling himself John Anderson has been taken by volunteers near Tarrytown and brought to this post. He claims . . ." Alternating waves of heat and cold pass through him. Blood rushes to his head. He reads on, learning that the papers found on the aforesaid Anderson have gone to his Excellency. All this while he is breakfasting with Franks and Varick! Arnold excuses himself, goes upstairs—his aides presume—to say good morning to his wife. Five minutes later a horse is heard galloping away. It isn't until half an hour has gone, when Varick enters his chief's office to confer with him about the day's instructions, that he finds the General missing; he assumes that General Arnold has gone over to West Point on a sudden errand, and tells himself that he will catch up with the General there in the course of the morning's duties. His Excellency General Washington and his staff turn up at Robinson's half an hour after this!

His Excellency may have a reputation for being cautious to engage the enemy, but he was evidently not slow to realize something amiss at Robinson's. No General Arnold to greet him. A report about the recent arrival of Lieutenant Allen from Jameson's. The papers he has received, taken from a man called Anderson who yesterday has written to say that he is Major André, the British Adjutant General, and which require some detailed explanation from General Arnold. Men are sent out at once to find the missing General. In a short while, a messenger returns: the General's barge has gone from its landing place on the riverbank. The guard there declares that the General had come not by way of the usual pathway but down a steep bank that would have unhorsed anyone else. He then commanded the crew of his barge to row him downriver on urgent business. He would have had the tide with him further down. No doubt he shot past Livingston at Verplanck's and if hailed would have called back something about going down under a flag; for himself he wouldn't have bothered to reply, but a pretense had to be maintained for the sake of the oarsmen until he was on board the *Vulture*. His Excellency then sends orders to Sheldon's at Salem that John André be brought at once to Robinson's, closely and narrowly watched.

September 30

When we got to Robinson's I was relieved to hear that Arnold had got away, if only just. As it was, my letter to General Washington might have arrived in time to have had Arnold seized, so slow had Lieutenant Allen been in providing the warning. So the entire house of cards had not yet fallen. Something might yet come out of this botched conspiracy to benefit Sir Henry and the King's forces. But while I thought this, I could not help at the same time feeling a fierce resentment that Arnold had left me in the lurch. He had kept very small his own risk while mine had been enlarged—and once again enlarged. And I was not the only colleague thus abandoned. Now Franks and Varick were clearly under a cloud. Moreover, soon after I arrived at Robinson's, while I waited under guard in the hall, an officer came from a side room; and looking in through the doorway I saw Joshua Hett Smith. He was sitting on a bench against a wall, hands clasped together. He was staring at the floor, and he did not see me. I wondered if he had made up his mind what to say. Would he plead guilty? Indeed, did he know whether he was guilty, and of what? As I looked at him, I decided that he had known what Arnold and I were involved in. But could it be proved against him?

The upstairs room to which I was eventually taken was in the addition to the house, and had a dormer casement window looking out over the garden at the rear. I was brought dry clothes, into which I changed. When I leaned out a little from the window I could see a few feet away the higher gable that formed the end of the main part of the house, and just beyond it another dormer, a little larger and higher than mine. As I stood there, a hand—pale and slim—grasped the sill of that neighbouring window. Perhaps I demon-

strated some sensation, for the young ensign whom
Lieutenant King or you, Tallmadge, had left with me
said, "I hope you are not intending to jump, sir."

"Oh, no," I said—and then, thinking at a gallop,
went on, speaking more directly out of the window,
trying to twist my voice towards the other window:
"Not at all. I'm merely taking deep breaths of the
morning air. How fine it is after the foulness of last
night!"

"You seem in good spirits, sir," said the ensign, a
trifle perplexed.

"Naturally I am in good spirits," I said, still speaking
in a voice that I hoped did not sound curiously loud,
but which would carry, as to the back of a theatre. "I
thank God for every moment of the day. Even this
present inconvenience gives me opportunity to recall
times past. I number among them quite a few enrap-
tured hours."

The silence behind me suggested that the young
officer might be wondering whether he should call for
advice; his prisoner was acting in a most bizarre
manner. Meanwhile, I watched the hand which was
suddenly stretched forth, palm turned upwards, a
wrist appearing and then the white cuff of a dress. She
had heard.

The cry of an infant came from that room; her
child, some five months old now, was with her, then,
and with perhaps a maid or a nurse as well. But she
remained at the window. Indeed, some of one forearm
in a cambric sleeve appeared, and then the other hand
and arm. The two hands clasped each other, seemed to
wring each other, in a gesture that I took to be one of
comfort to me or else a simple acknowledgement of
my presence. If there was someone in the room with

her, as there was with me, then there was nothing she could say, or dared say. But she leaned forward slightly, so that I glimpsed first the bodice of her dress, her hair, and at last her face as she turned towards me, so red around the eyes with weeping. She gave me a long, pitiful look, in which I saw both the child and the woman—the child perhaps sorry for itself, the woman for the man she looked upon. She formed her lips into what, could I have touched them, would have been a long and silent kiss.

"Yes," I said, still speaking as if to the garden and the woods around the house, "I am grateful both for the past and the present. The future remains a mystery, but is made easier to imagine when I consider that some of my old friends are, or will be, happy."

She closed her eyes, turned away, and drew back into her room. Possibly the child needed her, or her emotions had overcome her again. Ah, Peggy! Only to think, two years ago we were dancing.

I would have liked to have met General Washington. It is surprising that he has not been curious to see me; but perhaps he feared that too personal an attention to my case might affect the coolness with which he needed to determine what should be done, in justice and in policy. It was kind of you, Tallmadge, to give me a succinct report of the interview you'd had with his Excellency on the subject of John Anderson's venture, when you came to see me later that morning at Robinson's. And kind of you never to raise my hopes! And even kinder to allude to the situation of the young lady next door. I was—needless to say—fascinated to learn that General Arnold had made the swiftest of farewells, and had had time only to inform her that some transactions had come to light that must cause him to leave for New York at once. That one of the servants had found her in a swoon. And that this had been followed by a most frantic state, which had apparently lasted all day, and in which condition she accused those who came into the room of wanting to murder her babe. Her distress must greatly have affected those who saw her, and this response rebounded on the victim, since it was not until evening that the frenzy subsided. Young Colonel Hamilton, having spent much time with her, no doubt did not soon recover from the experience of female tears, of the misfortunes of beauty, of everything pathetic in the wounded tenderness of a young wife and the apprehensive fondness of a mother. Everyone at Robinson's was convinced that she was innocent of complicity in Arnold's deeds.

"What will happen to her?" I asked.

"She is being attended with every care."

"I mean, where will she go?"

"I understand that his Excellency proposes—perhaps it was Colonel Hamilton's idea—that she be sent to Philadelphia, to her father's."

I had thought of the girl in the next room. Seeing her for those few moments had made it remarkably difficult to think of her as Arnold's wife. And yet beneath that affecting girlish surface, I had no doubt, was a person as venturesome and resolute as the man she had married. Peggy Shippen Arnold had known what her husband had intended, I was sure. Her deranged and abandoned state may have moved his Excellency's young officers, but some of the emotion that lay beneath it sprang not merely from the sudden departure of her husband in traitorous circumstances but from the collapse of his plans and the capture and then appearance there of me. *I* would not be sent on to Philadelphia, from which city it would be simple enough to join the General in New York or London. But of course I made no suggestions aloud on those lines. Perhaps you, Tallmadge, had your doubts, too. You had not been at Robinson's the day before, the day of the performance, to be swept off your feet.

I did not see her again. It was after dinner when you took me, once more closely guarded, across the river to West Point. This was not how I had expected to observe the interior of this fortress, as a prisoner. Mr. Smith was in our little company, but avoiding my presence and avoiding my glance. A rather injured attitude appeared to be his, an impression of "I don't know how I came to be mixed in this, but I thought I was acting on behalf of the Congressional cause, doing what General Arnold had asked me to do, and how was I to know that this man Anderson was a British officer . . . ?" And now he was avoiding any further risk of infection by look or propinquity. I was tempted to unsettle him by directing my horse close alongside his and beginning a conversation about our ride to Crompond.

For some reason my spirits were not altogether low that evening at West Point. I let my mind dwell on the possibility of being exchanged, it could be for the American prisoners we held at Charleston. I was in a way reassured by the formal manner in which I had been recognized as an important captive; the proper forms were being attended to. I believed that Sir Henry, my commander, would by now have heard of my being taken; he would be deliberating as to what could be done to effect my release. Perhaps I could have my own Convention, in the fashion of Burgoyne and his army after Saratoga; perhaps it would be insisted that I take the next ship home and promise to serve no more in North America during these hostilities. It was notable how many officers of talent had in fact refused to serve here, believing it might be the death of their reputations and careers, not to mention the death that might meet them on the battlefield or during the sea passage. I knew some who had managed to go home on leave and then had striven to avoid being posted back again. Well, I can make promises as well as General Burgoyne. It might be a swift sail home.

In my mind I walked around London. I sauntered from one end of town to the other, from Hyde Park Corner to Whitechapel, avoiding only Whitehall. It is one of the finest of recreations, just strolling through a great city, despite the smoke and the stinks. The pleasures of seeing and being seen! To look in shop windows; to observe the activities of so many trades and professions; to cast a cool eye on the men and a warm eye on the women; to sit in coffeehouses reading the papers and to stand in inns conversing about the issues of the day with all sorts of customers. I will dine at the Mitre and take in a play in Drury Lane—I've yet to see Mr. Goldsmith's *She Stoops to Conquer*. When it comes down to it, despite my part-Swiss youth and my American maturity, I am a Londoner. I hunger for the park of St. James, for the river, for the piazza at Covent Garden, for the gardens at Ranelagh, for all the earning and spending and talk. I will take agreeable chambers in the Temple. When I am established, I will dine with Sheridan, but I think I will

now forswear my theatrical ambitions. Better to stand
for the Commons, and speak in the same assembly
with Mr. Fox and Mr. Burke. Then I can employ part
of each day in writing, perhaps in writing a history of
this present conflict, in which I will attempt to sup-
press my satiric tendency and emulate the great his-
torians of Rome, portraying some of our tribunes, for
example Amherst and Germain, in the light in which I
think posterity should see them. Writing, speaking,
sauntering—isn't this far better than a soldier's life?
And yet the military profession has been better than
that I had ahead of me as a young merchant. I have not
the slightest complaint.

What do you think, my dear Tallmadge? Have you
managed to read my canto on General Wayne? I
suspect, when you look at me, you find it hard to fit
the two characters together, the lighthearted versifier
and the ambitious staff officer. As far as I am concerned, they are compelled to coexist—one could not
be without the other. They are both I, but I concede
that the characteristics do not seem properly melded.
If they were, I would be more than I am. They contra-
dict each other at times; they interfere. Oh, to be a
man of single heart and mind and purpose!

On Wednesday night, at West Point, I woke in the
small hours and went to the window to look out. A
thin sliver of new moon appeared through the glass.
It is bad luck, my mother used to say, to see a new
moon so.

And on Thursday, the day before yesterday, when
you brought me down here to Tappan, I believed
finally in my ill fortune. It was you, Tallmadge, and
not the Board of Officers, that made it clear what was

to happen. Until then, although I knew what *might* and *could* happen, I had not fully recognized that it *would* happen, and *to me*. On Thursday morning many of the other circumstances of my life seemed to drop away, leaving just one determining factor. It gave me a lightsome, airy feeling, despite everything. To become hopeless was to become free. And what a day it was, floating in the barge downriver, in Arnold's wake but in less of a hurry, with the Hudson cliffs ablaze in colour, the sky a cloudless blue, the sultriness of September now almost gone and replaced by October crispness. Once we had got away from the place on the west shore where I might have landed Monday last, at the head of a select corps, I almost enjoyed the journey. I put out of my mind the approach I had intended up the mountain in the rear of Fort Putnam, which overlooked all of West Point. Once this key post had been taken, and with the troops of the garrison already dispersed by Arnold, the Point would have fallen. I stretched my arms out in turn over the gunwale, and dangled first one hand and then the other in the water. I watched the bubbles form in the wake of my fingers. The bubbles came into existence because of the forward motion of the barge and my fingers projecting into the still water, and they lasted for a few seconds before their breath expired, like so many lives, so many expectations. I ignored Smith, in the stern of the barge. He had tried to pass a friendly remark to me, and you had bade him keep silent. Poor Smith must have decided even before I did that my case was hopeless, and that his was different; he could afford a decent gesture to the hapless Englishman. And then, as we landed at Stony Point, we were met by the same soldiery that had been there when

Smith and I passed that way eight days ago. They came out to look at us curiously as we mounted the horses your waiting dragoons had brought there. I heard "Remember him? the man who had the touch of the ague!" I recalled that I had wondered, as I waited for the ferry to take Smith and me across to Verplanck's, if I would ever pass that way again, and if I should look at it as if for the last time. And now here I was again, and wondering the same thing. Surely there should be a statutory limit to the number of times one can be prompted to such sentiments. Of course I now felt the limit in my bones.

It was as we rode through Haverstraw that I felt the need to have you confirm this, Tallmadge, and thus asked you for your opinion about what would be my fate. How the subject alarmed you—how you shied away from it, said you would rather discuss the condition of the harvest in Connecticut or the value of the Continental dollar. It was not until we had stopped at Mr. Coe's house in Katiat, near the Clove, that you answered my politely reiterated question. I needed your opinion.

You said, speaking in a rush, that you had had a classmate at Yale College, by name of Nathan Hale. A much-loved friend. You had entered the Continental Army together in '76. Did I recall what had happened to Hale?

Ah, I did. But surely: "Our cases aren't the same, are they?"

Poor Tallmadge. But you gave me the honest answer: "I am afraid they seem precisely the same." After a pause, you added that his Excellency General Washington had a great antipathy to spies, though he employed them himself.

Major André

Before we rode into Tappan you must have seen from my countenance that I was no longer at my best. A cool breeze came from the north. Perhaps I seemed to shiver. You asked did I want anything? I confessed to feeling ashamed to enter the headquarters camp of your army looking as I did, shabby, unmilitary. My surcoat and cape had got left behind at Robinson's. I still wore Smith's bedraggled jacket. You had your servant bring me a dragoon cloak, and you insisted that I wear it. So I am not only a spy but a renegade. I rode into Tappan looking like an American.

I have been pursuing a thought back and back as far as I could do so. It is this idea that has, I believe, brought me here: the idea of fame, of glory achieved in the service of the King. Perhaps it is a small boy's ambition. Perhaps it is similar to the way a child seeks attention, or an actor wishes to be for a long moment at the centre of the stage, knowing the audience is entranced. In the nursery I had a child's rhyme book and saw myself doing what the characters of the nursery rhymes did, falling like Humpty-Dumpty off the wall, or getting beaten like Tom, Tom, the piper's son, who stole a pig. But naturally I felt closest to those heroes called Jack—Jack who was nimble and quick and jumped over the candlestick, and Jack Sprat, who ate no fat. Jack who went up the hill with Jill and then fell down and had his head patched with vinegar and brown paper. And Jack who built the house—"This is the cow with the crumpled horn, that tossed the dog, that worried the cat, that killed the rat, that ate the malt, that lay in the house that Jack built." Thus are we turned into devotees of poetry at the age of three or four. Most of all I liked the story of Jack the

September 30

Giant Killer. My father told it to me first. I made him and my mother recite it to me nightly till they were sick of it and I knew every word by heart. And I would tell it to myself as I lay in bed, waiting to fall asleep. I improved on it and enlarged it and embroidered it. A vine grew against the wall of our house, and a few leaves from it peeked around the frame of my window, allowing me to imagine that it was there for me to ascend, as Jack climbed his beanstalk. I was not scared of heights. I did not fear to look down, to see the roof of our house and the black holes of chimneys and the diminishing green patch of our lawn surrounded by flowered borders my mother tended. I climbed nimbly, like the other Jack—indeed, we are agile, we Jacks, no doubt because we eat no fat. Soon I was high enough to see the edges of Clapton, where the countryside begins, and soon I could see all of London to one side and the fields of Essex to the other, and then, higher still, I was in clouds and another country, all white, no colours at all. The hills, fields, and even the road were cloud-colour, and the castle that rose ahead was snow white, too. Here lived the giant.

All was quiet as I approached; the giant was asleep. I knew his treasure was stored in a strongbox, and I crept in along the stone-floored passage to the room where it was kept. The box was not locked. I opened it, and I was admiring the jewels and gold it contained when I felt a vibration in the floor. The whole castle shook. Grasping the box, I hid behind the door. I could hear him coming down the passage. "Fee fi fo fum! I smell the blood of an Englishman." My blood would be red as it spurted out; the whiteness of everything would be ruined. As it was by the giant's bulk, a black

[*155*]

shape filling the room, heaving with anger as he saw his box was missing. I took my chance and dashed out of the door and down the passage. I could hear him roar and begin to come after me. Crash crash crash. I ran across the courtyard, across the drawbridge. I clutched the box to my chest as I ran. I could feel the earth quiver and the air stir as the giant came behind me. I ran across the white fields. I had the tip of the vine in sight and reached it, began to clamber and slither down. Agile Jack! The giant had greater trouble in his descent and I managed to preserve the distance between us, though I could hear him puffing and ranting above me, screaming for my blood and his box of treasure. I got to the ground and ran into the garden shed, where an axe was kept for chopping kindling. It was short work to cut the great vine—four quick swings—the vine fell. A heaven-splitting cry from the air above, a vast black shape falling, a re-sounding crash, a huge dent in the earth. The giant slept forever.

People came from miles around to see the sight. There was a grand parade in my honour and the Lord Mayor of the City spoke. My mother and sisters and I were rich.

Sometimes I dreamed this story to the end. Sometimes, before the successful conclusion, I woke up screaming.

And now you want to know what the giant looked like. That is a penetrating query, Tallmadge. You know, I am not sure. Perhaps he was so gruesome, something like the cyclops Polyphemus, that I didn't dare look at him directly. He was noise and wind and the desire for blood. The cosmos responded to every heave of his breath. And when he had crashed into the ground, he was like a gigantic black bog; he became a deep morass that was barely discernible as giant-shaped.

I had a clearer picture of the honours I was awarded, the speech the Lord Mayor made, the friendly words of the royal personage before he dubbed me on the shoulder with his sword and said, "Arise, Sir Jack."

As you can see, my ambitions have not altered much.

I assume you have heard the news, Tallmadge? While you were out of the room just now, leaving Lieutenant King in charge, two aides of General Greene appeared. One announced himself as Major Burnet. They had come to tell me. It is to be tomorrow, Sunday, at five o'clock in the afternoon. My final ceremony. The end of ambition. Thus, twenty-four hours! I expect they will speed by, although I will do my best to rein them in. But in fact I am wrong to talk of the end of ambition. To live—that is a simple ambition, is it not? I admit to having a strong, concentrated desire to go on living. It is a desire which I recognize must confront—for the first time in my life—the fact that what is desired is completely without possibility.

A most astonishing thing has happened since you were last with me, Tallmadge, or it may be that King has already apprised you of the details. Another visitor followed Major Burnet, perhaps half an hour later. This was also a major, but he introduced himself in such a way that I did not catch his name, and I did not like to ask him to repeat it. He looked as if he was enjoying his errand even less than Burnet, who had managed to make his news-giving as formal, yet polite, as could be—though he hurried away without appear-

ing to take in my reaction. I imagine he had no stomach
for that. This second major hummed and hawed. He
sat down on that chair over there, having sought my
permission to do so, and wanted to know if I was being
properly looked after. Had I any complaints? Food?
Books? Paper and ink? It hadn't been a bad day, had
it? The air a bit closer now; perhaps some thunder
later on . . . By Jove, I thought he would start
chatting about his wife and children next, but he surprised me by telling me what he planned to do when
the present conflict was over. He wanted to run a
weekly gazette in some town in Pennsylvania. I truly
believed he would propose that I write him a column
or two for it; perhaps a canto dedicated to General
Washington; or "Thoughts of a Condemned British
Officer." But gradually he came round to his real
subject. There was, it appeared, a flurry of communi-
cations and deputations concerning myself going back
and forth between Tappan and New York. Lieutenant
General Robertson was in touch with General Washington and was coming upriver to meet General
Greene at Dobb's Ferry, perhaps this evening. But the
Major feared that General Robertson was merely
conveying General Clinton's previously stated claim
that I had been under a flag of truce and acting at
Arnold's behest—which I had already admitted to be a
hollow excuse, and not one I subscribed to. There was
also a suggestion from the American side that an
American officer now in British hands could be offered
in exchange for Major André.

I am afraid I cut the good Major short. What was
he leading up to? I had admitted the flag of truce was
not valid. Indeed, I was ashamed of having put it forward to begin with.

"I am leading up to this consideration," the Major said, looking like a man about to charge the enemy, and not pleased with the prospect. "It has been proposed that I put to you a possible way out of these unfortunate circumstances, which would facilitate your own release and the end of our own embarrassment at being under the, well, the present compulsion."

"Good God, sir," I said, "pray speak to the point."

He grimaced. "Our deputation to meet your senior officers tonight could take along a letter, if you cared to write it."

"That is most kind. And what should the object of the letter be?"

The Major was not enjoying himself. He looked at his hands. I took pity on him. There could be only one reason for this. It would be kindest if he did not have to say it.

"Major," I said, "there is not the smallest chance that Sir Henry Clinton would agree to exchange General Arnold for myself. If you think about it, you will see that it would not be good policy, whatever else it was in terms of conduct and morality. It would effectively dissuade any of your own men, officers or other ranks, from returning to what we regard as their proper allegiance. Which of them would come over to the King's cause if he believed that he might be sent straight back to you? In any event, Sir Henry has gained a good fighting officer. The balance of the arrangement, despite it falling disagreeably for me, is in his favour. And of course, in no circumstances would I consider proposing to my chief any action so demeaning, so dishonourable."

The Major sat there. He considered this. I thought he would leave after this conclusive declaration. But he continued to look at his hands, which were clasped together.

"As you can imagine," he said, "I do not regard this as a welcome duty. It was thought worth putting to you because we do not regard General Arnold as having acted in any way as an officer should. Furthermore, it might be considered that the arrangements he made, the measures he took, were such that his own security was paramount. If you had been surprised while talking together, it would have been in his power to sacrifice you. This remained so, and may have influenced the manner in which you were compelled to return to your lines. As it was—or so it seems to us here—you alone have been sacrificed."

"Put in that light, your remarks may be taken as an attempt to view me as an injured party, and for that, Major, I thank you," I said. "However, the light warps the truth, I am afraid. In no sense now can I blame General Arnold, or indeed Sir Henry Clinton, nor can I recommend any course of action to them. So if you will kindly convey those feelings to those who made this suggestion."

"Major André, my respects, sir."

He was glad to go.

Poor King looked dreadfully ill at ease and refused to meet my eye for some minutes.

Afterwards, of course, I went over that conversation again in my mind. I thought about how I could have written to Sir Henry—and what I might have said that would have tempted him to dispatch Arnold back upriver to his old friends. Perhaps it could have been done. But it would not do.

· · ·

September 30

Hamilton—what are you doing here? I didn't hear you come in. Have you been sitting there a long time? I think I was far away, in Lichfield again, strolling along the walk that runs between the cathedral and the abodes of the higher ecclesiastical dignitaries. That aisle of tall and venerable trees, haunted by the shades of great men who have walked beneath them. My shade, though a minor one, will perhaps saunter there. It is a consoling thought.

I assume you have been acquainted with the Major's failure just now, and I take it you are furious—yes, I see you seem to be—about the request he was asked to make. But rest assured, my pride is not severely hurt. Your attempt—and I mean the American attempt—to retrieve General Arnold by hook or by crook makes my attempt to restore him to the Crown less subject to criticism. But even if it had been your idea, Colonel Hamilton, to propose that I write to New York suggesting the exchange of him for me, I could not condemn you for it. All's fair. A touch of chagrin, perhaps, is felt by me that you would imagine the proposal stood the slightest chance of being accepted. But no—I absolve you. I can see it was not to do with you. Forgive me for the implication that it might have been. These hours demand a sharply honest examination of every action and motive, and given this, I admit that, were the positions reversed, I am not certain what I would have said had some British officer put forward the idea of making such a suggestion to you. Would I have denounced the man out of hand, damned him for his impertinence and questionable sense of conduct? Or would I have thought: Even so, it might be worth trying.

[*161*]

Major André

We have quite a lot in common, I believe. You worked in a business in the West Indies very similar to the one at which I slaved in London. You also have written—I gather Mr. Rivington published your pamphlet answering Bishop Seabury's attack on the Continental Congress. You speak French as I do. You serve your General in much the way that I serve mine. I have a feeling that you have viewed this conflict, as I have done for a long time, as a chance to exalt your station. And I wonder whether some wisdom is being acquired by you as it is, at last, by me. I am beginning to understand the differences that lie beneath our similarities on either side. You and your colleagues, I now realize, are not just Englishmen disaffected. You are people who have grown up on this side of the world, an ocean away from London, and your consent to government should have been requested, your participation required. We have imposed too much in defense of what we believed to be our rights. It may well be that you are defending the English principles better than we. Although whether you will go on doing so, if you win and in time become prosperous with the whole wealth of these shores, I beg leave to wonder. An excessive interest in land speculation and financial gain seems to be a vice not limited to merely one general. Your cry for freedom sometimes seems to be a cry for the right to make money untrammelled by responsibilities.

Some of these thoughts are, I admit, late to blossom. I remember thinking that our withdrawal from Philadelphia to New York in the summer of 1778 was a most successful movement—when in fact it now seems part of the confused and botched policy of dispersal, dictated by Whitehall, that has lamed us from the start.

September 30

I was at hand when General Grey, my former chief, told my present chief, Sir Henry, "A commander has more to dread from his employers than from the enemy." But given that Sir Henry had no inclination to evacuate Philadelphia, where we felt we were among friends, and that he knew our forces would be threatened along the route to New York, he handled the retreat most skillfully. We were not Burgoyned. At that time I was still aide to General Grey, and we were in the front sections of the march, which was led by General Knyphausen's advance guard. The army's baggage train was cumbersome, some twelve miles long, and all those wagons winding through the Jersey countryside made us most vulnerable. However, our discomforts could have been even greater at sea, where the French fleet was daily expected to remove our long-standing advantage on that element. We knew General Washington and your army were converging with us on the left, and I hoped that they would meet us in the van; but, as you know, it was the rear of our column that your advance guard under General Lee met at Monmouth Courthouse. I think I was well out of it that day. The heat made impossible a victory for either side. Even to keep marching, as our men did, was a triumph; to fight, to charge across those rugged ravines, was heroic. In our circles it was thought that General Washington was most unjust to General Lee in regard to his conduct that day; we felt Lee did wonders in holding our counterattacks and eventually withdrew in good order, and most certainly did not deserve the fate of a court-martial. Military justice works in strange ways!

That day we lost as many men through heat as through sword and shot. It is not a part of this country

I have any desire to revisit, at least in high summer.
Those scrubby pines, mile after mile; the dry sandy
soil, which reflects the heat and the glare, and provides
little shade and water. I choose the Hudson valley as
my theatre of war. I also have fond memories of your
islands off the New England coast. In September of
'78, after we were re-established in New York, I
accompanied General Grey on a foraging expedition
to Martha's Vineyard and the Elizabeth Islands.
Anchored in Holmes' Hole, at the Vineyard, we took
several hundred oxen and ten thousand sheep, and
collected from the burgesses the tax they had levied,
ready for sending to Congress. We then had to stay
over an extra day because two of our men had de-
serted; we got them back, poor devils, by threatening
to seize four of the inhabitants. I thought of Odysseus
and his men, for he had deserters, too, and was often
running into trouble when raiding islands for cattle.
But no Polyphemus appeared, and no Calypso or
Circe.

Food begins to occur in my meanderings, Colonel.
Will it soon be time to dine? My appetite survives. I
could do with oysters, mutton, and corn. When you
see his Excellency, please convey my thanks for the
many courtesies that are being extended to me. As you
can see, when I am not reminded of the present, as by
my stomach, my mind happily turns back towards the
past, avoiding thoughts of the immediate future. In
that direction I have only one request: I would be
happy—if it were possible—to be indulged the death
of a professional soldier.

Peter! I had not expected to see you here. What a
kind thought it was of Sir Henry's to think of sending

you; and an even greater kindness on the part of my hosts here to allow you to come. And I see you bring clothes and a change of linen, which I sorely need. My spirits are lifted by this—so come now, and don't look so low and desponding, or you will make me equally gloomy. I expect the news of New York, even if it is the gossip of your fellow servants. How is Lord Rawdon—as up and down as ever? Do you recall that time in Philadelphia when someone abducted his spaniel? How he roared and raved! Amazing how a man can become attached to a small beast like that. And Delancey? I haven't forgotten the rout we had at Hicks's before Sir William Cathcart's marriage, and Captain Delancey danced on a table, which promptly collapsed under him. Must lose weight, must Oliver. I hope you'll remember to give my compliments to Major Williams—Williams of the Artillery, that is—and my apologies that I won't be on hand to see him play Macbeth this winter. I had meant to do the scenery for him. There are some errands you will have to run for me, and bills to pay. I owe the bookseller behind Fraunces Tavern for the *Rasselas* he got me last month—oh, and for a copy of *Hoyle Improved*. I will write you a list, Peter, and give you instructions about which objects of mine to dispose of and who should receive certain possessions of mine. Meanwhile, bear up, man! These are details that have to be faced, and it will make things easier for my colleagues in the days to come if we consider them. You must particularly inform Captain Delancey that my wish was that he do his utmost to keep Sir Henry cool in the matter of my fate. I expect Captain Delancey to step into my shoes, as he gets on with Sir Henry. The fact that Sir Henry is now, as you say, in a rare old state, shouting at everybody and blaming himself, will not help matters; he will only damage his own interests in his choler. It will not assist Sir Henry's conduct of military affairs if he goes on in a harum-scarum manner, demanding revenge on General Washington and swearing that he will, if he captures him, hang, draw, and quarter the American commander. I fear, too, that he may blame General Arnold, and it will be better for our cause if General Arnold's military talents are immediately put to use.

Simcoe is another officer who should be properly employed. I am aware that as a Loyalist he knows the countryside well, and he is a venturesome commander of the Queen's Rangers, but although I am sure the motive was well-intentioned, whoever told you to mention Simcoe to me, and the possibility that he might take an ambushing party to the Philadelphia road, was thoroughly mistaken. I do not think I am leaving by that route, my good fellow. And an even greater difficulty with this sort of talk is that it tends to broaden horizons. You see, I am already getting used to the fact that my world has shrunk to a small space, as big as this room, and is on the point of becoming smaller still. At this stage, Peter, I do not want any hopes, any prospect of what might happen other than what I am certain *will* happen. Resolution is what I need, and possibilities are no help. The right mood, if I can gain and sustain it, is one of acceptance of my lot. This is contrary to what has always been my natural optimism, to look forward to good fortune and a general improvement of things. Mr. Johnson has some memorable lines in his *Rasselas* to the effect that misfortunes should always be expected. The angels of affliction spread their toils alike for the

virtuous and the wicked, the mighty and the mean—
and presumably for those, like myself, in between.

Did you bring any books? No matter. Colonel
Hamilton here has promised to lend me some, some
others—I assume—than the works of Citizen Paine
and Ambassador Franklin. I have a craving to read
Robinson Crusoe again and perhaps dip into some of
the history plays, like the *Henry IV*s. I am filled with
a strong sense of fellow feeling with the fat old
knight brought down by foolishness. But I am not
certain how much time I have for reading. There are
several letters to write tomorrow. And I would like to
make a sketch or two.

Will you arrange my clothes, Peter, so that my
dress tomorrow evening is faultless? We must be seen
to do our part as well as we can. There is little left to
do except work to improve our final by-command
performance.

TAPPAN

Sunday, October 1

1 7 8 0

I woke this morning, Tallmadge, quite sure for a moment I was somewhere else. I was late. I would have to dress in a hurry and run to the office in Warnford Court. Great mountains of account books awaited me, more threatening than a firing party. Lines of figures parading, marching, and countermarching. But here I am—my business life nearly recaptured me—it is a lucky escape! I suppose I should have a special feeling on this morning: a last dawn, a last hearing of birdsong, but I don't note any particular sensation in that way. I breathe as usual. I rub sleep from my eyes. I scratch my ear, my chin. I await a visit from your barber to remove this bristly feeling. The body does not yet recognize that it will shortly cease to create a need for these customary exercises. Its parades and manoeuvres are to end. Surely it should envy constitutions like yours, whose blood will be warm tomorrow, whose senses will perceive and hear and feel; which will stir from sleep, wake up from dreams. Constitutions belonging to those who will have dreamed, and will know they have dreamed.

I have been out in the garden for a while with Lieutenant King—with sentinels correctly posted at the gates, of course. I walked the bounds. I watched the maple leaves come adrift from their boughs and float downwards, rocking through the air. I watched a fuzzy orange-and-brown caterpillar working its way over a fallen leaf, arching its back, straightening out, arching its back, straightening out—each segment of motion taking it forward a little. It did this until it reached the topmost edge of the leaf, obviously saw the great drop that greeted it if it went further, and turning to one side, came down the leaf to the grass again. What was the purpose of that mission? Was it wasted time? Did the caterpillar enjoy its journey up and down the leaf? Will it avoid such leaves from now on? Or will the blackbird which was chirruping sweetly in the maple tree remove any opportunity for choice, any chance of the caterpillar making a decision in this matter, by following the fall of the leaf and, in one swoop, snatching the caterpillar in its bright yellow beak? Crunch—gulp—soon gone. Does this make the caterpillar's voyage all the more pointless? Or are we looking at it from the wrong point of view? Perhaps neither the caterpillar nor the blackbird has a choice. A primal hunger moves them both. But the caterpillar found no food on its journey, and the blackbird did.

Meanwhile, I admired the warm colour of the trees and the cloudless blue of the sky. I think you are fortunate with October here—it came today and you'll have a month of it. There is a feeling of the land storing up the last heat of the sun to see it through the winter—all that red and gold and umber. In my next life I shall be a painter, or a blackbird! In England we are often made to feel that we are on an island; the clouds come in low, grey, and wet, full of ocean.

October 1

This land gives instead the impression of spreading westwards without limits, on a scale that ought to make man feel humble, though it often seems to have the contrary effect. Perhaps it is gardens that provide the right intensity of vision, where we watch the making and unmaking of things and see ourselves as part of the same process. The fall of the leaf. It will become part of the ground part of the grass next year, and in time soil where a new tree may be born. As you can see, I am adjusting my ambitions still.

Now I must stop daydreaming and occupy myself.

I have written several letters since I breakfasted. It is damned difficult, you know, to write in these circumstances to family and friends. One must try to cheer them up, imagining the frame of mind they will be in when the letter reaches them. One has to get beyond the debilitating barrier that when they read the words one is scribbling down the writer will be no more. How that empty gulf yawns and stretches towards one! It is our foreknowledge of the abyss that sets us apart from the blackbird and the caterpillar. How pleasant it would be to abdicate this human eminence and *not* know, and simply be struck down without warning. We have to face in advance the terror of death's great emptiness, square our shoulders, and twist our mouths into a cheerful smile. I have thus twisted my words to my mother and sisters and hope that the letter does not read like a grimace.

I have tried to convey to them that I am not unhappy; that I am well treated; that I have been given every consideration. They are not to be ashamed of my death. A punishment is made ignominious only by the crime it is attached to, and I do not think it a crime to have attempted to end a civil war and to have tried to prevent the further effusion of human blood. I have told them whom to approach to obtain my will, which I made on Staten Island in '77. I have left most of my funds to my sisters and my brother, Bill, on condition they provide some additional income to my mother during her life. My childhood friend Walter Ewer is to look through my papers, manuscripts, and drawings, and should feel free to destroy or retain whatever he thinks right to do. My mother has the advantage of a strong religious belief, which will be a consolation to her at this moment. She will pray for my soul; she will count on meeting me in the hereafter. And I think she has been more or less prepared for news of my death since I took my commission, certainly since I came to these shores. In a way, this is dying in action, is it not? If my family see it that way, it will not be so painful for them.

And yet, despite having written to them in this spirit, I feel in truth less sanguine. I am terribly afraid that the mode of execution your friend Hale suffered will also be mine. It is a shameful mode, suited for common criminals, for highwaymen and thieves—and for spies, I know, under our rules, though I cannot feel that such an occupation was mine. I have been properly tried and judged, and with the verdict of the Board of Officers I have no dispute, but the possibility of being hanged fills me with unmitigated dread. I am thereby declared to be at fault in a way I know I have not been. I am made at one with those who commit arson or murder, with pirates and highwaymen. Anyone who has grown up in London as I have has seen gibbets frequently enough, by the banks of the Thames, at Tyburn, or on the heaths and commons surrounding the city. Sometimes the gibbets are mere empty frames, gallows of lashed poles or of beams treenailed together, awaiting their next victim. Sometimes the last occupant hangs in them still, in chains, birds pecking at him. I have never looked closely at the sight. I have averted my eyes as I passed by. Since I have been in the army, I have of course had to witness executions. There was a soldier of the 52nd, hanged for desertion; two men of Lord Cornwallis's force, a light infantryman and a grenadier, shot for plundering. I hope that I will be shot. A death in action. Surely General Washington cannot refuse me this.

My Uncle Lewis took me to Tyburn once when I was seven or eight. Possibly he imagined it would be a great treat for a small boy. The occasion was the execution of an eminent highwayman. Hanging days are public holidays with us and the streets were thronged, all the windows filled with people looking to see the cart go by, carrying the prisoner. I forget the malefactor's name, but he had paid some men to follow the cart as mourners, wearing the proper hatbands and gloves. He himself wore an elegant coat, had a huge nosegay in his buttonhole and a string of rosettes at his knee. I can see him still. How the crowds cheered him—you would have thought him a general who had won a great battle, or a king going to be crowned. When he climbed the ladder set beneath the gibbet, he had a flower clenched between his teeth. He looked around at the crowd. I felt his gaze light upon me.

Kind Uncle Lewis! I dreamed about that experience several times thereafter. On hearing my shouts, my mother would come to my bedside to soothe me back to sleep again. But it did not need to be a dream; some nights, before falling asleep, I saw him climb the ladder. It was Jack, grown up; the youthful giant killer had become a highwayman. He was also something of a dandy. He climbed the rungs slowly but easily, the flower in his mouth, and then turned to look at me. His hands were tied behind him. The noose was put over his head and tightened around his neck. Finally he spat out the flower and, still gazing at me, was just about to say something—something I needed to know—when the ladder was tugged away. He did not fall far. He swung. He bobbed and swayed. And he did not go quickly but struggled in the air, his feet thrashing, seeking support they could not find. The crowd was silent, and some who had come to look looked away. I kept my eyes upon him unwaveringly. I wanted him to burst his bonds, for the noose to break and let him fall. But the noose held, and gradually his shakings and heavings ceased; his face darkened. It took a dreadful long time. Then his feet were still.

I think Uncle Lewis thought of it as a form of blooding, which would also be a spectacle for a boy.

I heard that General Washington once reprieved a soldier—one of your own—from execution on the day appointed for the sentence to be carried out. Was that the case?

Minutes are passing.

Now I will draw.

As a pastime, it has the advantage of making the mind go blank—no, that is not exact: the blankness is one in which questions are being asked and answers made, but they are in a different sphere of things from ordinary thought. They have to do with the pressure of one's fingers on the quill, with the motions of fist and wrist, with the way—looking at the mirror on that wall—I regard the thousands of lines and lights and shadows in order to determine which to use in the portrait of myself; which few will speak for many. It is a self-regarding task in which self disappears because of the necessary concentration and application, the visual and physical duties that the task demands. And the result is this perhaps not perfect likeness that yet contains something of me, for I have put part of myself into it, and that will last a little longer than me. Will you look after it, Tallmadge, or see that it goes to someone who might like to keep it? A keepsake.

That reminds me—I owe some money to John Ramage, the portraitist in William Street. He was painting a miniature of me that I meant to send home. I must put a note on the list for Peter to take to New York. For Delancey: Pay Ramage. Miniature to Mother.

I have written this note to General Washington, which perhaps Lieutenant Tomlinson or Ensign Bowman could take over for him to consider if they are not otherwise engaged. I have not sealed it—you may read it if you like. It is a modest plea, a request from one soldier to another. I do not ask to be spared, but simply to have the manner of my death adapted to my feelings. What I hope is that his Excellency could show that no resentment is here at work against me—rather, the precise operation of military practice. This may require me to die but might yet allow him to inform me that I am not to die on a gibbet. Knowing this would soften my last moments. It would also cause less anguish to my family when they come to hear of it.

But perhaps there *is* resentment, and an obstinate need to show no mercy. I can see that in some lights this will be seen as an act of sovereignty. From what Hamilton told me, I believe that it is felt that they must proceed even at the expense of their own feelings.

Tallmadge, tell me how you imagine this conflict will come to an end. A great battle? Or simply exhaustion on both sides? We have been tempted south by the milder winters there. We continue to follow a mistaken policy of dispersal, injudiciously dividing our army into numerous detachments and carrying on operations in several colonies at once. Cornwallis, despite his recent successes, for example against Gates at Camden in Carolina, is ill supported; as usual, the countryside has disappointed our hopes that it would rise to join us against Congress—one reason being, of course, that we are known to evacuate a post not long after taking it, thereby abandoning the loyal people to their bitter enemies. During these marches through the country, the spirit of depredation is too often prevalent among our men. Sir Henry has realized that there is little point in taking land we cannot hold. He would prefer a war of raids and to hold in reserve the ability to strike a forceful blow when permitted. But Whitehall drives us to adopt other policies. Plans they dream of one year we have to try to effect a year later, when much has changed. And now the arrival of the French has swayed the balance sorely against us; we find ourselves fighting at sea against several powers. It seems unfortunate that a King, Parliament, and people who are opposed to the ancient despotisms of the Continent should find themselves at odds with those who are sprung from the same roots, their own cousins, who inherit the same passions and prejudices. But we have been affected by this kinship. We have never

been able to treat you as out-and-out enemies; we have
not been ruthless, as victory in war demands. We have
always regarded you as though one day you might
become our friends

Beyond Pine's Bridge the road followed the Croton
river southwest, winding through small hills. Bumpy,
irregular country, with much marshy ground and only
the occasional cleared field. The few farmhouses along
the way appeared to be abandoned and shuttered up.
Weeds grew high in their gardens. Fifteen miles to the
White Plains. I came to a junction with several
cottages, a horse trough, and a well, where a small boy
was hoisting a bucket. Jupiter dipped his muzzle in the
trough. I held out a coin and asked the boy about
the roads from here. Had anyone been past so far this
morning?
"You don't mean any of us from hereabouts?"
"No. Armed men."
"Three volunteers went down the Tarrytown road
within the past half hour. But the White Plains road
has been empty, at least so far as I could tell."
"Good lad," I said, tossing him the coin. I set off
along the road to the White Plains.

Lieutenant King has just brought me a copy of the
afternoon orders. It appears that my end is postponed
until tomorrow at noon. Concerned parties are still
to-ing and fro-ing between here and Dobb's Ferry
and New York. But I cannot imagine that these dis-
cussions will alter my fate. Although I hunger for
every minute gained from oblivion, yet I do not welcome the delay. My mind was fixed on five o'clock this
afternoon. Terminus, the god of boundaries, will be

annoyed that the limit of my life has been shifted when it seemed so firmly arranged. And now his Excellency will have to show his generosity and kindly send me one more breakfast from his table. I shall do without dinner tomorrow, I am sure.

Consolations, Tallmadge—I have been thinking of certain problems of life that I will now be able to avoid. I have got through to this point without being smitten by the smallpox, and will need to fear it no longer. It will not blemish my skin. I will not grow bald, or lose a limb in combat. I will not have to kill anyone. Do you know, I have come this far as a soldier, despite being in several actions in which my sword was drawn and used in the heat of battle, and have not taken another's life to my knowledge. Indeed, in the night raid on Baylor's Dragoons here at Tappan two years ago, I saw that a whole troop was spared death. I will be spared the indignities of old age, of disease and disrepair. I remember Uncle Giradat, Lewis's older brother, as he became senile and incontinent. He did not remember his friends or family; he shook and he smelt. Hardly the kind of old age we venerate. I will have no problems with drink, debt, or distraint, and all preoccupations with rank and estate will cease to worry me. Will Sir Joshua paint me? Will I gain a knighthood? Will the King summon me to an audience at Kew? My country house. My wife and children. No anxieties in those respects.

You observe that my regimental jacket has arrived. It came from Belmont, where it was found in a search of Mr. Smith's house. I am gratified to have it again, even if it represents a turning point in this brief

odyssey that I do not care to be reminded of. Peter
has cleaned and pressed it. I will be properly dressed
for the occasion at midday tomorrow. I understand
that eighty files from each wing of your army will
be in attendance, so as a martial ceremony it should be
stirring. At least there will be nothing furtive about it:
the practices of war are being demonstrably adhered to.

It will be a comfort to wear my jacket.

All asleep, or dozing. Tomlinson, sitting in his chair,
his eyes shut, his head falling forward from time to
time. King or Bowman in the other room. But the
sentinels alert in the garden, pacing past the window.
Starlight, moonlight. The sky is like a great colander,
with the light of heaven shining through the holes. Is
there anything behind it other than light? It seems
likely that when I have left this world I will find
myself in nothing. Yet I cannot comprehend nothing,
or nowhere, or a void. I suppose some of my fears arise
because of the darkness ahead of me, the uncertainty
of what it is, and because I know for certain there is
no coming back. That is the fear of the future, or its
lack, and the other thing is the dread of giving up
what is past, of loss, of a world ceasing to exist for me
of which I have been a part, and will no longer experience when my thoughts and perceptions are blotted
out—when my senses, in a last tumultuous shaking,
dissolve for all time. But musket shot will make it
quick.

I have been trying to read *Tristram Shandy* again
this afternoon—Hamilton's idea of a work that would
entertain me at this juncture. If only I could stretch

out my dying as Tristram stretches out his birth, with such digressions! With accounts to reconcile, anecdotes to pick up, inscriptions to make out, stories to weave in, traditions to sift, personages to call upon, and panegyrics to paste up at this door. My memory—though the word is too precise—of my own birth is one of rush rather than procrastination. It seems to me that it must have been like falling through the air, with a great rush of wind. I imagine this on the basis of what blood and bone seem to remember, as if recalling what has formed them, or perhaps on the basis of what they foretell—for my departure may be similar. Homage to life's symmetry, if nothing else.

If I had retired home with a wound like Uncle Toby, would Peter have served as my Corporal Trim? Then instead of a model of the fortifications of Namur, I would have had one of West Point, with plenty of scarps and counterscarps, batteries, revetments, saps, ditches, and palisades. Our siege of Charleston earlier this year was too rapidly successful, and our engineers have been deprived of the opportunity to conduct such works. I would have limped about my battlements while Peter made sounds of bombardment and cries to indicate the movements of our men as they enveloped the enemy positions. I would whistle jauntily for both sides, "Lilliburlero" for the attackers, "Yankee Doodle" for the defenders. Music to keep the spirits high. Or sing the way Wolfe did:

> *Why, soldiers, why*
> *Should we be melancholy, boys?*
> *Why, soldiers, why,*
> *Whose business 'tis to die!*

October 1

Like all soldiers, I knew that I risked death in the King's service. Like all soldiers, I believed that it would not come to me.

It is a nuisance, dying, in this respect, that it is hard to get it out of one's head. Everything is now related to it. I find it impossible to have a thought unconnected with it. For example, if I perform the humblest service to myself, such as blowing my nose, I wonder if this is the last time I will blow it. Every event becomes hypothetically a final one; one's mind is crammed and overwhelmed by so much finality. And one wonders if it colours one's judgement of other matters. I was thinking just now of Honora, and suddenly I was conscious that she was dead. Is this because I need company in my misfortune? Am I trying to carry her along with me now, having been unable to make such an attachment in life? These doubts spring from me because I know that death is besieging me and I am unable to shake it off. But I believe my sudden vision is true. It came in a shaft of bursting clarity, like sunlight from a high window in a church illuminating an inscription on the stone floor: HONORA SNEYD EDGEWORTH. She is gone. The dear girl was never strong. The flush in her cheek, though beautiful, was a token of danger. She was thought to have had a brush with consumption at fifteen, and escaped. Dr. Darwin feared for her then. Miss Seward wrote to me four or five years ago that Honora was having trouble with her vision—I think this was not long before she married Richard Edgeworth. Honora will have known the nature of her disease, and that it was incurable. I must try to summon up, for my part, a calmness equal to that I know Honora will have shown in the face of death, while holding on, to the last, to a manly observance of those small kindnesses and acts of fellowship that make life so agreeable.

I wonder if I should stir Tomlinson and ask him to take a look at the clock in the anteroom. It must be midnight. I have not the faintest desire to sleep. There will be plenty of that soon.

TAPPAN

Monday, October 2

1 7 8 0

But I have been dozing. This must be the case, for otherwise this rigid member would have been the result of conscious, lustful speculation. How ramrod firm it is! And yet I remember no amorous dream. It appears that the force remains that brings us into being; the procreative urge lasts to the end. Well, old fellow, you hold up well. Maybe you will make such a salute in the concluding moments. Hurrah to life! Hurrah to love! I haven't given you much opportunity for manoeuvres these past weeks. True thoughtfulness on the part of his Excellency would consist not only in sending me breakfast but in arranging for other comforts. "See that Major André is allowed a little rogering before he goes to eternity." Ah, the door opens behind the snoring Tomlinson. Someone has slipped by the guards and comes towards me. I hear her dress rustle. She stops, tantalizingly, just beyond the point where the faint incoming light can reach her. I have to go to her and, putting my fingers under her chin, tilt up her face to look at it. Her arms are around my neck, her thighs are against mine, her tongue is between my lips. Drickje. "Dear Jack." Dear Drickje. I seek that close and thrilling rapture of the senses that will blot out the onrush of the ogre who is pursuing me, seeking my blood.

Perhaps the Sewards and Mr. Sneyd were right. Perhaps Honora did the right thing, choosing Edgeworth. Perhaps I would never have married. I am a man for the lightness of love, not for its heavier, steadier courses. When it comes to it, I wonder if the bosom that I would now like to be pressed into, even hide within, is not maternal. As if my mother could save me from what waits.

I will not inform on you, Tomlinson. Sleeping on duty! The light of day has just broken. Yes, I have had a peaceful night. A few sweet dreams. Daydreams, you might call them, except that they occurred in the small hours. A few fancies and visitations. Oh, and I have been here and there, travelling around. There's no holding me down, you know. I am a restless fellow, have been since my childhood years in Geneva gave me a second home. Not that the Switzers would recognize me as one of their own, but the Alpine peaks enthrall me as much as do our soft and swelling Surrey and Sussex downs. I have been walking the terraced promenade at Lichfield and cantering down Broadway and watching a small boat sail away across Lac Leman. I have been climbing vines or beanstalks. I called on Sir Henry just now; he was in his nightshirt, but delighted to see me.

"We've been missing you, André," he said. "Can't think how we'd get along without you. Old Arbuthnot has been thoroughly exasperating me—doesn't seem to understand that we are engaged in hostilities against the French. He's meant to keep an eye on the movements of their fleet, but his eye is often shut. Now, what do you recommend we do with this new chap, Arnold? Mrs. Baddeley says I should let him loose against Congress—send him up the Schuylkill with a fleet of gunboats and cannonade the whole scoundrelly mob."

General Phillips was there, too. He had come up from the Chesapeake, looking very pale. In fact, he was shaking terribly with fever. He was quite down on Earl Cornwallis and thought that his policy of rapid movements through the Carolinas and into Virginia was absolutely mistaken. Fever and the French would attend him, Phillips said. Sir Henry is generally pleased to hear criticism of the Earl, but he did not seem happy at this. I then thought I caught a glimpse of a pair of figures hovering nearby. They listened. They spoke a few words in French. One looked to me like your General Washington, but he kept his face concealed. A dark cloak. I tried to alert Sir Henry, but he paid no attention; he didn't seem to hear me anymore. General Phillips said, "Don't worry, André. It'll all sort itself out in the end."

I was hoping you had not given up on me, Tallmadge. Will you breakfast with me? I am also hoping that you will be able to tell me if my letter to General Washington was well received and let me know what he has decided. I would like to be acquainted with the manner of my death. Will I be shot or hanged? I would have thought you might have known by now and in that case could have told me, realizing how uneasy I am on this score. I assure you, you do not spare my feelings by evading an answer. However, I do not mean to pester you. It must be difficult for you. In any event, I do not think it will be the suspense of

not knowing that kills me. Pray, never mind. But I
would be glad to know.

*Permit Mr. John Anderson to pass the guards to
the White Plains, or below if he chooses, he being on
public business by my direction. Benedict Arnold.
Major General. September 22nd.*

I went behind the lines. I took off my coat. I carried
papers.

I want to die like a professional soldier.

This is going to be the most difficult thing I have
ever done in my life.

Mutton chops for breakfast. A bottle of wine. It
looks, it tastes, like claret. "Here's to the French alliance!" My tongue still has the power of taste; my jaw
still works; my teeth still bite. Is it true that young
Lafayette has his own cook? You would think a
people with such standards in food would manage
better in the way of kings. But I must eat and drink
lightly. I have a shameful fear of not being able to
control my body's functions at the end. How we are
seen to behave is generally taken for what we are.

So, sir, you are the minister here, the acting chaplain
to the American Army at its Tappan camp. It is civil
of you to come. Acting chaplain to acting adjutant
general. No, I am smiling because . . . because I have
never been a very religious fellow, in a churchgoing
sense, but I recognize in myself a grateful response for
this gesture having been made to me, and for the fact

that my soul is receiving attentions that my body may not. And yet curiously I am not ready for the consolations of religion. Perhaps body and soul have to be in a more receptive, possibly run-down state. It seems to me that I am readier at this moment for the sort of offer made to Faustus. If Mephistopheles materialized at this instant and promised me continued life in return for a waiver of any chance I might have of entering heaven, I would sign his contract immediately. A bird in the hand. Especially when reports on the nature of the bush are so confused and uncertain. No, I don't think the horned one would impose other conditions on the arrangement. What conditions had you in mind? Joining the American Army, perhaps, as a fair trade—as you would call it—for General Arnold? I'm afraid that wouldn't do at all. I would expect Mephistopheles to allow me to keep my present rank and office under the Crown.

Prayer? As you will. I feel my mind tending towards flippancy when it should be more composed, more dignified, thinking of calmer things. Eternity is not calming, however; not yet, at any rate. Canon Seward used to preach a sermon that dwelt on the beneficent ease of the hereafter, the bliss of the Elysian fields following the stress and strains of life, but it never convinced me. But if we are going to pray I would prefer to kneel. Our Father, which art in heaven . . . deliver us from evil . . . for Thine is the kingdom . . . forever and ever. So be it. My mother taught me how to pray, how to hold my hands. "You must close your eyes," she'd say, "and think of what you would like God to do, and ask Him to look after you and your brother and sisters." "Can I pray for Walter, too?" I said. "Of course you can." And I prayed that Walter's parents would allow him to come to the fair with me and that we would win a coconut and see the fat lady and eat sugar apples. That I would get a kite for Christmas. Prayer is eminently selfish much of the time, in my experience. But perhaps if I had known that Honora was dying, I would have prayed for her. I would have addressed a plea to Whomever, to Whatever, to the Power that presumably set this impossibly inscrutable universe in motion, and would have asked Him or it to deflect by the merest smidgen the momentum of destiny that was about to obliterate Honora. But knowing full well that such adjustments are of no interest to the Supreme Being—that we are like caterpillars, or drops of water, in most respects, indeed, in all respects except that of being conscious of our beginning, our middle, and our end. We have a small amount of control over the course the middle passage takes. But we have little control over the end, unless we decide to kill ourselves and thus have the privilege of choosing our own manner of departing the world. The privilege of the brave. Or is it braver still to face uncertainty with composure? I will try.

I have been watching the sunlight on this table, the edge of shadow slowly, imperceptibly moving across the brown back of Sterne, across the white paper on which I have been sketching. The window frame creates the effect of a sundial. Time is the movement of sunlight and shadow. It cannot be fastened down. I wonder how long this drawing will last: a man rowing ashore from a sloop-of-war anchored in Haverstraw Bay.

. . .

October 2

A final evacuation. Sitting in the privy, Tomlinson
and guards outside. The contemplative ridiculousness
of a man with his breeches around his ankles. A blackbird chirping vehemently from a nearby tree. There
is an ounce of comfort in having him for a neigh-
bour. Bird, tree, and earth. I will nourish them; they
will be me. Meanwhile, practical matters, like the
doing up of buttons, persist.

Peter, you will have to get a grip on yourself. This
lamentation doesn't help. Besides, wielding a razor at
my chin while shaking with sobs is not in the interests
of military justice—you will finish me off before the
announced time. You must show them that a British
soldier is made of stronger stuff. Concentrate on holding the blade at the proper angle to the skin, on gliding
it down my cheeks in a smooth, clean motion, and
wiping it before the accumulation of soap and whisker
becomes so heavy it falls onto the floor or onto me.
Gravity. I don't suppose it possible that that particular
natural law will be suspended today. But if you attend
to the details and duties of assisting me, you will better
get through this last hour. When you arrive at the top
matter, please dress my hair simply—you can tie it at
the back with a plain black ribband. I asked Lieutenant
King for one, and he will give it to you.

And, Peter, I want you to have my clothes. Lean on
the table if you are going to start trembling again. I
can't wait for you to stop shaking, man: these things
have to be said. You must preserve my regimental coat
for your children and perhaps their children. "This
belonged to Major André," someone may say. And
there will follow a few tales. One thing, however, is
not for you. My cravat. Will you deliver it to the

Major André

King's Arms, at the corner of Whitehall and Bridge Street. To Mijnheer Stoutenburg's serving girl, Hendrickje, at that address. If she asks, tell her I was thinking of her at the end.

When does the tide start to ebb today? Just after midday, if I'm correct. That is fitting. Tallmadge, I am glad to see you again. The time approaches, I presume. I can hear your men forming up outside, and someone was trying out his drums just now. A firing party—how I hope for it, see it in my mind! It will be the swiftest and most decorous conclusion. If I think hard enough upon it, it may just happen that way; wishing may make it so. The row of men, the muskets aimed, the command, the stir in the air—I will not even hear the noise of firing. Now, Peter, hold my coat and I will slip my arms into its nicely tailored sleeves. *I* will never take it off again, I assure you, Tallmadge. That is a lesson I have learned.

So I am to have companions on the walk, I am glad of that. King. Bowman. Arm in arm, then. It is an aspect of soldiering that people in ordinary life don't understand, what friends we are in those times we are not shooting at or bayonetting one another. We comprehend the risks we all take, the feelings we each have. Yes, I am ready to go, as ready as I ever shall be. Thank you for the room, the bed and board these past days. My compliments to his Excellency. To a degree, the rule of military law diminishes the savagery of our conflict, don't you think? I am attempting to keep out of my mind any thought that there might be, at the last moment, a reprieve. I am ready to march forth. King and Bowman, you must not let me falter. Peter, goodbye, good man. Don't worry about me. It will be but a momentary pang. And Tallmadge, my gratitude to you is great. If you have the chance, tell people that I was not a coward when it came to this.

The last doorway. And then sunlight. Files of men. Martial music. A light breeze. King's arm. Bowman's arm. They squeeze me so that I feel my own blood thundering. Feet sound on gravel. The way ahead lies open between the ranks paraded on each side upon the grass. A puff of white cloud over the hill, the trees— the gibbet. Sweet Christ! To be throttled, after all, like a common criminal! It affects my breath already. My eyes blur. The men in the front ranks have on their faces tears that sparkle. Dear grass—gravel— cloud. Hold up then, Jack. Climb up then, Jack. Wagon or vine. Chin up, then, Jack. Ah, such a hush for the Colonel's statement. Tallmadge out there, watching me. No, I can do it myself, by your leave— there's a silk handkerchief in this pocket. Feeling of silk. Eyes darkened but still a taste in the mouth, rough and salty. Isn't this silly? I seem to stand on the edge of the stage. My voice would carry to the back of the hall, to loud applause. The noose is tight under my chin. The rope is coarse. Loud and black is the wind, the vine falling, falling, falling. *Jack.*

E N V O I

Colonel Tallmadge resumed: "I thus had the honor of commanding the officers and men who guarded Major André while he was held captive. I was impressed by the fact that Major André's behaviour was candid and correct throughout his confinement. During the many hours I spent with him, he devoted much time to gazing through the window, pacing the floor, reading, and sketching. Although manifesting every sign of politeness and even friendship, talking to me as if we were men who had served together, he did not unburden himself in any unseemly or impolitic manner. I believe he was most concerned about the effect of his arrest and sentence upon other people connected to him. When the time appointed for his execution arrived, he came to the door of his room wearing his bright scarlet regimental coat, buff vest and breeches, and with his hair tied with a black ribband at the nape. He was met by Lieutenant King and Ensign Bowman, who linked arms with him on either side. The escorts—myself, Captain Russell, Captain Hughes, and Captain van Dyke—marched behind. Six hundred men were drawn up along the route in files on each side; many were weeping. An inner guard formed a square around the place of execution. As we marched forth, the band of the Pennsylvania line played "The Bluebird." A number of the senior officers who had served on the Board preceded us on horseback. His Excellency was not present. It was about one quarter of a mile to the place, and as we set off Major André seemed immensely calm, nodding or smiling to officers he recognized; but when he caught sight of the high gallows that had been set up on the hill he was unable to repress his emotion. "Does it have to be this way?" he asked. Captain Russell told him that it was unavoidable. (I was unable to speak, ashamed that I had not had the courage to tell him before how the execution was to be carried out.) Major André did not falter in his step, however, and eventually he smiled, recovering his composure, and said that although he was reconciled to his death he detested the means of effecting it.

"The gallows had been constructed of poles, two at either end forming a fork at the top in which a cross-piece rested. In the middle of this, a rope had been fastened. A horse-drawn wagon was drawn up beneath. When Major André saw that all was ready, he climbed quickly onto the wagon by himself. Colonel Scammell, who was in command of the execution, read out the Board's sentence and asked Major André if there was anything he wished to say. I could not meet Major André's eyes, but I felt he glanced at me as if to remind me of words he had addressed to me earlier; he said, 'Nothing, thank you, other than to ask that you all bear witness to how I meet my fate.'

"His voice was constrained, but I admired his ability

Envoi

at that moment even to speak. He walked once back and forth along the wagon, as if testing the way it had been built, and then took off his hat and laid it down. He looked around at the surroundings and the mass of soldiery. The hangman, one Strickland, his face and hands covered with pitch, stepped forward with the halter and attempted to put it over Major André's head, but Major André stopped him with a politely raised hand. Major André unpinned his own collar, removed his cravat, and then, taking the halter, put it over his head, placed the knot under the right ear, and drew the noose snugly to his neck. He then took from his coat pocket a white silk handkerchief and tied it over his own eyes. The perfect firmness with which he acted melted our hearts. Colonel Scammell in a loud voice commanded that Major André's arms be tied, too. Major André, though blindfolded, reached into the other pocket and produced another handkerchief, with which his arms were tied slackly, just below the elbows, behind his back. His face was pale, his lips tightly pressed together, but he remained composed.

"Colonel Scammell raised his sword. It glinted in the air for an instant, then flashed down. Strickland, holding the reins, tugged the horses forward; the wagon rolled; Major André fell. He swung back and forth but made no struggle. After half a minute Colonel Scammell directed one of the inner guards to go forward and bear down upon Major André's shoulders, to ensure that he was not long in agony. His face was swollen and black when he was cut down. Apart from the one moment in this whole affair in which Major André showed no presence of mind or wholehearted attention to duty—thanks to which our cause was not dealt a fatal blow—his behaviour inspired admiration and esteem in those of us who met him. He was an engaging man, and a brave one, and I remember him often.

"Major André's servant collected his clothes."